The Royal Guest

The Royal Guest
and Other Classical Danish Narrative

Translated and Edited by
P. M. Mitchell and
Kenneth H. Ober

The University of Chicago Press
Chicago and London

P. M. Mitchell is professor in the Department of Germanic Languages at the University of Illinois, Urbana. Among his publications are *A History of Danish Literature, Anthology of Danish Literature,* and the English translation (with W. D. Paden) of three tales in *Carnival: Entertainments and Posthumous Tales* by Isak Dinesen, the latter published by the University of Chicago Press.

Kenneth H. Ober, who received his Ph.D. in comparative literature from the University of Illinois in 1974, is assistant professor in the Department of Foreign Languages at Illinois State University and the author of *Meir Goldschmidt.*

The University of Chicago Press, Chicago 60637
The University of Chicago Press, Ltd., London

Printed in the United States of America

Library of Congress Cataloging in Publication Data
Main entry under title:

The Royal guest, and other classical Danish narrative.

CONTENTS: Goldschmidt, M. The Battle of Marengo. Maser: an episode from Simon Levi's life.—Jacobsen, J. P. Mogens.—Pontoppidan, H. The royal guest.—Bang, H. Franz Pander. Expelled from Germany.

Includes bibliographical references.

1. Short stories, Danish—Translations into English. 2. Short stories, English—Translations from Danish. I. Mitchell, Phillip Marshall, 1916– II. Ober, Kenneth H.

PZ1.R7647 [PT8024.E5] 839.8′1′301 77–78070
ISBN 0–226–53213–5

Contents

INTRODUCTION
1

MEIR GOLDSCHMIDT
The Battle of Marengo
25
Maser: An Episode from Simon Levi's Life
34

JENS PETER JACOBSEN
Mogens
79

HENRIK PONTOPPIDAN
The Royal Guest
133

HERMAN BANG

Franz Pander
197

Expelled from Germany
218

NOTES
237

Introduction

What particular claim does Denmark have on the attention of readers of imaginative literature abroad? What are the virtues of Danish literature that one should turn one's attention to it? To these questions there are straightforward answers. For the last several hundred years Denmark has been an important cultural entity in Europe. It has produced numerous writers possessed of incisive minds, penetrating imaginations, and striking means of expression. Through belles lettres, Danish authors have addressed themselves obliquely to the great problems of human existence and have provided interpretation or solace or both. They have written from an awareness of a common national cultural heritage, although time and again, they have received the strongest impulses from abroad. They have felt a sense of responsibility and an inner need to depict what they have observed and to interpret the past historically or psychologically. Within the context of Western culture, the problems of life in Denmark are basically those of life in other countries. The messages and convictions which one deduces from the novels, short stories, poetry, and plays of Danish writers are transferable to other Western cultures. Were it only for the philosophical quality which informs Danish writing of the nineteenth century, however, one could make no claim to special importance within the realm of imaginative literature, but the leading Danish writers of the nineteenth century have also been masters of language and style. They have combined vision with a mastery of metaphor. When one reads them, one does not quickly forget what one has read. They may, therefore, be said to possess characteristics of writers who have claim to an audience that is not necessarily restricted by the narrow borders of a small linguistic community.

Prior to the eighteenth century, Denmark made few contributions to what we call world literature, that is, imaginative literature which has an appeal beyond the borders of its country of origin. In the eighteenth century, and notably through the work of Ludvig Holberg (1684–1754), the kingdom of Denmark and Norway began to produce a vernacular literature which appealed not only to readers of Danish but—chiefly through the medium of German translation—also to the outside world. Holberg acquired fame for his comedies and, to a lesser extent, for his satirical verse, his histories, and his essays, but no vernacular narrator of international stature had yet come to the fore. The impact of the new novel emanating from England was felt in Scandinavia, as elsewhere in Europe, and generated imitations. The important and original literature of eighteenth-century Denmark was, however, not narrative prose. Other than Holberg, the leading writers of the century—Hans Adolf Brorson, Johannes Ewald, and Jens Baggesen, among others—were primarily poets, although Ewald and Baggesen each left an important prose work best classified as travel literature. At the turn of the nineteenth century, there was a new and enthusiastic Danish imaginative literature inspired in part by the new German literature and philosophy of the 1790s. This new Danish literature, which, above all, is associated with the name of Adam Oehlenschläger (1779–1850), was expressed primarily in the form of poetry and plays. Various prose works in German and English were widely read in the original and in translation, especially works by Goethe and by Sir Walter Scott. More than Goethe, Scott encouraged imitation, but the novels of a would-be Danish Scott, B. S. Ingemann, can make no claim to international attention.

There was, nevertheless, a provincial outsider among the Danish writers of the early nineteenth century who was a notable storyteller: Steen Steensen Blicher (1782–1848). Blicher, who was miscast in life as a Jutland clergyman, produced a large number of novellas, some of them utilizing historical motifs and many of them reflecting life in the Jutland countryside. His production is admittedly a jumble of wheat and chaff. Nevertheless, it is not too much to say that, in Denmark, Blicher is the best-loved domestic writer, principally because of his unsophisticated national orientation. He might well be represented in the present volume, were it not for the fact that his most important stories are already accessible in English translation. It is curious to note that Blicher's best-known tale, which in English is called "The Journal of a Parish Clerk," drew on the biography of the same seventeenth-century Danish woman who became the title character of Jens Peter Jacobsen's novel *Marie Grubbe* half a century later.

The nineteenth century is spoken of as the golden age of Danish imaginative literature and art. During the first three-quarters of the century, there arose numerous writers who produced for Danish readers an entire library of lyric poetry, narrative, and drama. Some of these writers made names for themselves abroad as well as in Denmark. While Adam Oehlenschläger and Johann Ludvig Heiberg are little known today outside Denmark, they were part of the active European literary scene in the first half of the nineteenth century. Oehlenschläger wrote both in Danish and in German and had many readers in Germany. Heiberg was, on the one hand, involved in a controversy with the German dramatist Friedrich Hebbel and, on the other, was the guiding spirit in Danish literature, the man who launched the careers of both Hans Christian Andersen and Søren Kierkegaard in Copenhagen. There is no need to belabor the point that Hans Christian Andersen and Søren Kierkegaard themselves achieved world stature, for the names of both have practically become household words the world over. Several other writers have maintained an audience within Denmark. The most important is the many-faceted genius N. F. S. Grundtvig (1783–1872), poet and prophet, best known as Denmark's most prolific writer of hymns and as the founder of the folk-high-school movement (which was the progenitor of adult education). The somewhat younger Frederik Paludan-Müller (1809–76) produced between 1841 and 1848 an epic poem, *Adam Homo,* which, among all works of Danish imaginative literature, can best be compared with Goethe's *Faust.*

Modern Danish prose does not really become established until the publication of works of lasting value by Hans Christian Andersen, Søren Kierkegaard, and Meïr Goldschmidt in the 1840s. Andersen (1805–75) had clearly demonstrated his ability as a storyteller as early as 1829 with the publication of a humorous volume which purported to describe a walk from a part of Copenhagen to the island of Amager on New Year's Eve in 1828, but he did not elect to pursue the genre at that time, since he wanted primarily to be a playwright. His plays were only moderately successful, and in 1835 he turned to writing both novels and the tales which are inaccurately identified in English as "fairy tales." The grotesque and fantastic element apparent in his work from 1829 on is missing in the novels, which tend to be descriptive and autobiographical, whereas fantasy is the basic characteristic of the tales. At first, the novels were more widely acclaimed than the tales, but after publishing his second volume of tales in 1843, it was clear that Andersen had found his most successful and rewarding medium. While he continued to write in other genres, including travel literature, he is known outside of Denmark today almost solely as a writer of tales. It would be inaccurate to identify Hans Christian Andersen's tales with the developing current of Danish narration; his point of origin was the folk tale, but the genius of his work is his own. The enthusiasm and naiveté which permeate his tales are peculiar to him rather than to his times.

Like Hans Christian Andersen, Søren Kierkegaard (1813–55) commands an international audience—but for different reasons. He is a theologian, a thinker, and a philosopher, who is also a master of diction and of irony. Some of his works are cast in narrative form—the best-known example is his magnum opus *Enten-Eller* (*Either/Or*)—but his works cannot be subsumed merely under the narrative heading. While his appeal and impact to a large extent derive from his command of devices used by imaginative writers, what is ultimately important in his works is his existential religious message. Since Andersen and Kierkegaard are readily accessible in translation, there is no compelling reason that they be included here—but one might also ask whether or not either writer can be said to typify classical Danish narrative prose. Kierkegaard and Andersen are, rather, anomalies.

The third great writer of the 1840s, Meïr Goldschmidt (1819–87), does not share the international prestige of his contemporaries Hans Christian Andersen and Søren Kierkegaard. Although he cannot be said to possess the profundity of Kierkegaard or the appealing naiveté of Andersen, he nevertheless warrants attention from the outside world. To anyone who is familiar with Kierkegaard's life, the name of Goldschmidt will be immediately identifiable as the merciless critic of Kierkegaard and editor of the satirical periodical *Corsaren* (The Corsair). Such an identification is, however, grossly unjust to Goldschmidt, who, after his early sallies in *Corsaren,* became a master of narrative prose, and who as a writer of novels and short stories in Danish had no superior during his own lifetime. Goldschmidt is the most important Jewish author that Denmark has ever produced. He was a realist before realism became the parole of the day, and he dealt with social questions before Georg Brandes had given his charge to a younger generation that it make social problems a matter of debate. Goldschmidt's greatest contribution is his novel *En Jøde* (A Jew, 1845). In this novel, which was autobiographically tinged, Goldschmidt depicted with accuracy and perception the life of Jews in contemporary Danish society. Nowhere before had the Gentile world had such access to intramural Jewish life as an enclave within European society. The book was a revelation, for it removed the screen, as it were, from between the home life of a Jewish-Danish family and the outside world. It was soon translated into English (two different translations, published almost simultaneously) and German. Yiddish and Russian translations followed.

While *En Jøde* established Goldschmidt's name as a writer on Jewish subjects, he wrote three other novels not primarily concerned with Jewish materials. These were the monumental *Hjemløs* (*Homeless,* 1853–57), *Arvingen* (The Heir, 1865), and *Ravnen* (The Raven, 1867). Goldschmidt's own English version appeared in 1861.

Goldschmidt is of special interest to readers of English, since in 1861 he moved to England with the intention of establishing himself in Victorian London as a writer of English. Besides *Homeless,* his English writings consisted of shorter prose works and were published in the major London literary journals of the day. Although he gave up the venture and returned to Denmark in 1863, his published English writings represent no mean achievement in the literary world of Dickens, Thackeray, Bulwer Lytton, and Disraeli.

Goldschmidt's shorter prose works fall into several categories. There are Jewish tales, non-Jewish tales, and travel sketches. While the Jewish tales are generally the most interesting, simply because they depict, without the tendency to caricature, the life of an exotic element in Western society, numerous of the other works are intrinsically valuable. As a writer, Goldschmidt demonstrates himself to be quite as much a Dane as he is a Jew, and in numerous of his sketches there is no Jewish element, whereas there is great intimacy with Danish life and the Danish landscape.

The two short works here translated represent two vastly different aspects of Goldschmidt as an imaginative writer. Neither has appeared before in English. "Maser" is the best of Goldschmidt's Jewish tales and depicts his greatest and most unforgettable characterization, Simon Levi, who first appeared in the novel *Ravnen* and there played a crucial role in the unmasking of the villain and in the consequent triumph of the heroes. Simon Levi was apparently so popular with Goldschmidt's readers that the author could not resist devoting a short story to him. Unlike many sequels, the story surpasses its parent work. The tale is one of the best demonstrations of Goldschmidt's sympathetic, humorous, and gently ironic treatment of his favorite character, who is irresistible in his shrewd, Talmudic, hair-splitting honesty. "The Battle of Marengo," an earlier piece, shows, in contrast to some of Goldschmidt's writing in *Corsaren* (especially that which appeared during his feud with Kierkegaard) that his satire was not always biting or cruel; indeed, that it was at its best when it was in a milder vein. The title refers to the village in northern Italy, near Alessandria, where Napoleon decisively defeated the Austrians on 14 June 1800.

Although the literature from the early decades of the century enjoys a fixed historical position, it is, with some exceptions, little read, compared with the prose literature which sprang up in Denmark in the second half of the century—and especially that which was published after 1871, the year that marked the beginning of critic Georg Brandes' epochal lectures on the main currents of European literature at the University of Copenhagen. This does not mean that all Danish works published before 1871 are to be relegated merely to literary history or that Brandes actually introduced a new literature. The hymns of Grundtvig are, after all, still sung in Denmark, Frederik Paludan-Müller's *Adam Homo* is still read; the fairy tales of Hans Christian Andersen are as much alive as any other piece of world literature; the works of Søren Kierkegaard continue to attract attention in many countries; and works by Meïr Goldschmidt continue to be read in Denmark because of their intrinsic and not merely historical value.

In treating Scandinavian (and not only Danish) literature of the nineteenth century, literary history has tended to establish a dividing point around the year 1870, the so-called breakthrough of a modern, internationally oriented literature, and to view the works that were produced subsequently as superseding earlier literature of much less importance. The flaw in this assumption is indicated quite simply by the fact that Brandes was himself lecturing and writing on the literature produced prior to 1870.

The short stories and novels which began appearing in Danish in the 1870s and the 1880s are new, however, in that they consciously incorporate ideas imported from abroad which were being expounded by Brandes. Political and social movements affect their form and means of expression.

Of the Danish writers represented here, Jens Peter Jacobsen (1847–85) is the writer associated with the Brandesian "breakthrough" who is best known abroad. He is considered the greatest Danish stylist because of the care which he employed in his descriptions and particularly in his use of adjectives, especially those pertaining to color. He is, however, also a perceptive psychologist. By profession a natural scientist (he translated Darwin into Danish), he has a small production because of his prolonged illness and early death from tuberculosis. He wrote only two novels, a handful of short stories, and a few poems, but his entire oeuvre is still alive, and his novels continue to be read widely in Danish as well as in translation. One of the novels, *Marie Grubbe*, which carries the curious subtitle *Interiors from the Seventeenth Century*, was published in 1875, and was both hailed and condemned as an example of starkest realism. We would say today that the realism lies in the great detail of Jacobsen's descriptions and in the psychological portrayal of the major character, an historical figure who has been treated in various ways by other Danish writers.

Jacobsen's other novel, *Niels Lyhne* (1880), is set in the nineteenth century. Although it also is a psychological novel, it deals with the problem of achieving a life philosophy. The major character is an agnostic or atheist, who ultimately meets his death on the battlefield without perceiving life to be anything but chaos.

Jacobsen established himself in Danish literature through the publication of "Mogens" in 1872. It was as if this story were the direct response of a creative mind to Georg Brandes' demand for a new literature. "Mogens" contains a great deal of action, but it evoked attention in particular because of its descriptions, especially for its introductory paragraph which has been cited again and again as an example of effective naturalistic portrayal.

Unlike Herman Bang and Henrik Pontoppidan, Jacobsen has fared well in the English-speaking world. Translations (by Hanna Astrup Larsen) of both of his novels were published between 1917 and 1919; both have been reprinted several times. An English translation of "Mogens" appeared in 1921 together with some other stories by Jacobsen. Because this earlier translation (by Anna Grabow) leaves much to be desired in the way of accuracy and the representation of Jacobsen's style, a new translation was undertaken for the present volume.

Nothing attests Jens Peter Jacobsen's international appeal more strikingly than his popularity in Germany. There are no fewer than ten different translations into German of *Marie Grubbe* and seventeen different translations of *Niels Lyhne*. There are, moreover, seven translations of the collected short stories and four editions of Jacobsen's collected works in German.

It is a curious coincidence that three of the foremost writers of late nineteenth-century Denmark were born in 1857: Henrik Pontoppidan (d. 1943), Herman Bang (d. 1912), and Karl Gjellerup (d. 1919). They were, however, but three of a generation of important writers of prose and poetry, who came to the fore subsequent to Georg Brandes' lectures at the University of Copenhagen in the 1870s. Pontoppidan and Gjellerup were to share the Nobel Prize in 1917, but of the two, only Pontoppidan is read widely today. Gjellerup wrote much of his later work in German. Even in 1917, it seemed a trifle odd that Pontoppidan had to share the prize with Gjellerup.

Pontoppidan has the greatest appeal of the Danish writers of the late nineteenth century, not only because he is a skillful narrator and is able to depict both in vignettes and on broad canvases the conditions which obtained in Denmark from the 1880s and 1890s through the first two decades of the twentieth century, but, above all, because he is able to depict the struggle for a personal philosophy.

As a writer, Pontoppidan was at first a social critic in the spirit of Georg Brandes. He started by depicting, somewhat sentimentally, the life of common folk in the country, particularly of those who had suffered unjustly at the hands of society. The naturalistic doctrines of milieu and heredity were clearly recognizable in his work. He matured quickly, and in a collection of short stories entitled *Skyer* (Clouds) in 1890, he expressed indignantly and ironically, but wittily, his wrath at the dictatorial provisional government of J. J. Estrup, who was the authoritarian prime minister of Denmark for over ten years. The stories in *Skyer* have long been viewed as classics by Danes, especially the tale entitled "Ilum Galgebakke" ("Gallows Hill at Ilum"), in which Pontoppidan castigates his fellow countrymen, as exemplified by the rural community whose chief spokesman is a Grundtvigian nationalist, for their failure—out of deference to the status quo—to rise up and make their wishes known.[1] The stories in *Skyer* are caricatures based on the contemporary scene, as suggested by the subtitle, "Sketches from the Days of the Provisional Government."

The desire to give a picture of the times as well as to tell a coherent tale informs Pontoppidan's trilogy *The Promised Land*, for each volume bears the forthright subtitle *A Picture of the Times*. The major character of *The Promised Land*, one Emanuel Hansted, is a clergyman who, while serving as a chaplain in a country parish, breaks with the traditional and conservative ecclesiastical practice of his superiors and attempts to identify himself with the rural population. He marries a country girl, but despite the early promise of their marriage, it, like everything else that Emanuel Hansted undertakes, gradually goes downhill, and Emanuel shows that he cannot really disassociate himself from the sophisticated culture in Copenhagen from which he has sprung. After he and his wife have parted

1. A translation by David Stoner is found in *Anthology of Danish Literature*, bilingual edition. (Carbondale: Southern Illinois University Press, 1971, pp. 332–59 [paperback ed., 1973]).

and he spends some time in the capital, he returns to the country even more of a dreamer and fantast than before and ultimately sees himself as a reincarnation of the Saviour. He has lost his mind—as had his mother before him. The message of the influence of heredity and milieu is clear.

It is noteworthy that there are some parallels between events in the life of Emanuel Hansted and of Pontoppidan himself. Most significant was Pontoppidan's marriage to a country girl in 1881 and the dissolution of that marriage ten years later under circumstances which are reflected in his novel.

Pontoppidan's magnum opus, *Lykke-Per* (Lucky Per), which appeared in eight small volumes between 1898 and 1904, is also a picture of the times, but the slow and painful progress of the major character toward the achievement of a personal philosophy of life is the underlying theme of the entire work. This character, Per Sidenius, has many traits in common with Pontoppidan. When one reads Pontoppidan's autobiography, published toward the end of his life, one finds elements that are recognizable in *Lykke-Per* as well as in some of his other works.

Like Pontoppidan, Per Sidenius is the son of a Jutland clergyman. He wants to become an engineer and be among those who, in the name of technology, are building the future. Per is, however, unwilling to obtain the necessary training but is driven by ambition to sketch a huge project for a new harbor and waterways for the area around his hometown in Jutland. On this and many other counts, he is not true to himself. He also compromises himself in dealing with several women to whom he is attracted. He pursues material gain by seeking marriage with the daughter of a wealthy Jewish household in Copenhagen, but the proposed marriage, like all his grandiose plans, comes to naught. He has gambled by compromising himself and lost. Ultimately he does not escape his heritage; he returns to Jutland and marries the daughter of a rural clergyman. For a long time he remains unable to face reality, and only by sacrificing all worldly goods as well as his family life does he finally achieve a personal philosophy and peace in his own mind.

Still a third multivolume work, entitled *De Døđes Rige* (The Realm of the Dead), was published between 1912 and 1916. Even more than *The Promised Land* and *Lucky Per,* this work endeavors to give a picture of the times and a social interpretation which would throw light on all aspects of life in Denmark in the early years of the twentieth century. Society is seen to carry a burden from the past and to be hampered by many common weaknesses of human character which prevent the development of a healthy and self-confident society that is willing to carry the responsibilities for its own actions and to maintain its integrity. The mood of the work is pessimistic, for it does not seem that life is really worth living under the conditions which Pontoppidan depicts.

Pontoppidan's last novel, entitled *Mands Himmerig* (Man's Heaven, 1927), is an exposé of life in Denmark at the beginning of World War I, with particular emphasis on the role of the press in society. It is a further example of belles lettres used as historical tapestry, but it lacks the impelling quality of the earlier works.

In addition to the works mentioned above, Pontoppidan wrote many short stories and short novels between 1881 and the early years of the century, of which "Den kongelige Gæst" (The Royal Guest, 1908) may be considered a good representative. The events of a single evening, which allow hidden wishes and desires of the characters to come to the fore, are enough psychologically to make a difference in their continuing existence.

To the end, Pontoppidan was the most lucid of Danish writers. In five small autobiographical volumes which appeared between 1933 and 1943, the year of his death at the age of 86, he provided a kind of "Dichtung und Wahrheit" about the first five decades of his own life. He permits the reader to draw numerous parallels between some of his characters, especially Per Sidenius, and himself. Although Pontoppidan's novels are pervaded by an air of pessimism and the tragic, there is an indomitable spirit of hope and optimism in the autobiography. While Pontoppidan may not believe in the perfection of man, he does believe in man's ability to create a better world even in the face of the holocaust of World War II. On this count, he differs from the naturalists Jens Peter Jacobsen and Herman Bang, the former of whom takes no position with regard to the improvement of man, although, as a Darwinian, he must have believed in progress; and the latter, who depicts only a heartless world in which the sensitive and pitiful individual perishes.

Although Herman Bang had published considerable literary criticism prior to 1880, it was with the appearance of his first novel, *Haabløse Slægter* (Hopeless Generations), in that year that he left an indelible mark upon Danish literature. The book was suppressed by the police, although the reasoning for such action seems incomprehensible to us today. The novel depicts the degeneration of a family. A parallel in Thomas Mann's first great novel, *Buddenbrooks,* which was published twenty-one years later, immediately comes to mind. The theme of degeneracy is not uncommon in Herman Bang, and is suggested by Bang's own *fin-de-siècle* spirit and unhappy life. Degeneracy connotes a kind of overrefinement, an overrefinement which is tragic and out of place, as can be seen in Bang's short story "Franz Pander" taken from his collection *Exotiske Noveller* (Exotic Tales), published in 1885.

There is a second predominant theme in Herman Bang—that of the pitiful and wasted life. This theme is expanded with greatest poignancy in Bang's novel *Ved Vejen* (By the Wayside, 1886), which relates the colorless, piteous existence of the sensitive wife of the gross manager of a railroad station—and employs a kind of stream-of-consciousness technique which was to come into its own only in the twentieth century. In his later, more impressionistic works, Herman Bang is important for another stylistic reason. For the first time in world literature, he created the impression of multiple conversations being carried on simultaneously—an effect achieved by the use of incomplete sentences and interwoven, unrelated snatches of dialogue. The novel *Stuk* (Stucco, 1887), to which he refers (as he also does to *Ved Vejen*) in the sketch "Udvist af Tyskland" (Expelled from Germany, 1891), is a monument of impressionistic style, whereas *Det graa Hus* (The Grey House, 1901) represents the high point of his phonographic—one might say tape-recorderlike—technique.

It is difficult to understand that such masters of the narrative art as Henrik Pontoppidan and Herman Bang have remained essentially unknown in the English-speaking world. Only one of Bang's novels—*De uden Fædreland* (*Denied a Country,* 1906), has appeared in English; it is inferior to several of his other works, although not without interest because of the autobiographical quality of the book. Only two-thirds of one of Henrik Pontoppidan's major works, *Det forjættede Land* (*The Promised Land,* 1891–95), appeared in English translation—at the end of the nineteenth century. A few short stories were also translated, but have long been inaccessible. This fact is the more surprising in the case of both Bang and Pontoppidan, for they have been widely translated into other languages and have enjoyed considerable popularity, particularly in Germany.

Although he is not represented here, simply because numerous of his stories already have appeared in English translation, Johannes V. Jensen (1873–1950), a Nobel Prize winner (1944), must also be mentioned as an outstanding literary figure from the turn of the century. Jensen plays a triple role in the history of Danish literature: he was a poet, a writer of short stories, and a novelist. In each genre, he made remarkable contributions. He is most widely read today as the author of short stories, the first collection of which, *Himmerlandshistorier* (Himmerland Stories, 1898), contains sketches of life in that part of northeast Jutland which is called Himmerland. Two more collections of tales from the Himmerland appeared in 1904 and 1910, respectively. Jensen was not merely producing regional literature, however, although the setting was a limited area in rural Denmark. He subsequently wrote a large number of other sketches and short stories which were gathered under the title of *Myter* (Myths) and issued in five collections between 1907 and 1924. Jensen himself felt that he was a latter-day Hans Christian Andersen and that his so-called myths were, in a way, a continuation of the tales of Andersen. He believed that he was "concentrating on those short flashes of the essence of things" and not telling short stories in the ordinary sense of the term.

In 1906, with the publication of a collection of poems which were in part inspired by Walt Whitman, Jensen introduced a new spirit into Danish poetry. In his poetry, as in his novels, Jensen was wholly anthropocentric; he was an admirer of technology, and he looked to the New World for the culture of the future. His magnum opus is the series of six volumes which bear the common title *Den Lange Rejse* (*The Long Journey*, 1908–22), an attempt to depict the rise of man from the Ice Age until the discovery of America by Christopher Columbus. The novels combine narrative skill with a popularization of anthropological knowledge and the Darwinian theory of evolution—with an emphasis upon early man in Scandinavia.

More widely read than Johannes V. Jensen outside of Scandinavia is Martin Andersen Nexø (1869–1954), known primarily for two long novels, *Pelle Erobreren* (*Pelle, the Conqueror*, 1906–10) and *Ditte Menneske-*

barn (*Ditte, Child of Man,* 1917–21). Both novels, masterpieces of modern Danish narrative, are litanies of injustice, which attest the profound political and social convictions of their author, who shared a social realism with the early Henrik Pontoppidan. The novels have been translated into several languages, including English. Andersen Nexø's works have enjoyed their widest distribution in the Soviet Union, where they are said to have been issued in over five million copies. Andersen Nexø wrote his first stories and sketches in the late 1890s, but few of the shorter works may be considered to be on a par with his novels, chiefly because they are dominated by a tendentious social quality.

There are at least two other writers of Danish prose from the second half of the nineteenth century who have a claim to a lasting position on the Danish Parnassus, although critics would scarcely grant them equal standing with the authors represented in the present collection. Vilhelm Topsøe (1840–81) was a writer who furnishes a parallel to the Brandesian "breakthrough," although he was independent of Brandes and, with a few other writers, something of a foil to Brandes. In his earliest work, one already finds the kind of narrative prose for which Brandes was agitating. In 1875 Topsøe published a realistic novel entitled *Jason med det gyldne Skind* (Jason with the Golden Fleece), which is spiritually related to the novels of Jens Peter Jacobsen and Herman Bang, although its roots antedate Brandes' lectures.

Gustav Wied (1858–1914), finally, is an outstanding ironical humorist in Danish literature, who is still widely read, especially because of the novel *Livsens*

Ondskab (Life's Malice, 1899) and the sketches from the collections *Silhuetter* (Silhouettes, 1891) and *Barnlige Sjæle* (Childish Souls, 1893). These serve to remind us of the strong undertone of humor in Danish literature, humor which can be perceived in all the writers represented here except Jens Peter Jacobsen. Wied mixes his humor with a drop of wormwood, however; the tendency to disillusionment evokes sadness as well as laughter. Like the other great Danish writers who have been mentioned here, Wied is quick to perceive and deride the hypocrisy which is so pervasive in daily life.

There are not a few Danish writers of the twentieth century who presumably will achieve lasting fame, but it is too early to bestow the epithet *classical* upon them, since we lack the objectivity which only the passage of time can grant. If a work of imaginative literature is to be labeled classical, it must possess at least three essential characteristics. First, it must be able to hold the interest of succeeding generations of readers. Second, it must give evidence of the author's mastery of language—diction and the figures of speech. Third, it must concern a situation which readers can envisage on the basis of their previous experience or observation. A work which is to have any claim to an international audience some decades after it is written must be able to transcend its own time and the cultural entity of which it was originally a part.

These are difficult requirements to meet, and only a small percentage of the imaginative literature produced in any one country since the victory of literacy —and the concomitant rise of the public library about one hundred and fifty years ago—can be said to have any claim to a continuing audience either at home or abroad. Considering the size of the country, Denmark might be thought to command more than its share of attention within the sphere of world literature, if only through the works of Hans Christian Andersen and Søren Kierkegaard. We have observed, however, that several other relatively well-known names have some currency among the educated readers in the Western world. It remains a moot question whether or not some of these writers derive importance merely from the fact that they are Danish and represent Danish culture. In whatever way this question be answered, the fact remains that there are numerous other Danish writers who have a claim to international stature either because of the attention they already have evoked from readers in countries outside Denmark or because of their demonstrably intrinsic value. An example of the former would be the works of the bilingual writer Karen Blixen, or Isak Dinesen, as she called herself in English (1885–1962). An example of the latter is Frederik Paludan-Müller's untranslatable epic poem *Adam Homo*.

The four writers represented in this collection have a firm place on the Danish Parnassus. That is, they are not literary curiosities and do not command attention out of piety. They are artists who have been able to keep an audience for succeeding decades—in the case of Meïr Goldschmidt, for well over a century; in the case of the others, somewhere between 75 and 90 years. They deserve to be made available to the English-speaking public.

Meir Goldschmidt

In his memoirs, *Livs Erindringer og Resultater* (Life's Recollections and Results, 1877), Goldschmidt included "The Battle of Marengo," which he said he had found stored among some old papers. He could not remember exactly when it had been written, and he claimed to have a modest opinion of its literary worth. The title refers to the village in northern Italy, near Alessandria, where Napoleon decisively defeated the Austrians on 14 June 1800.

"Maser" was first printed in 1868, as part of the collection *Smaa Fortællinger* (Little Stories). The collection appeared first in fascicles, the last of which was published early in 1869. "Maser" enjoys continued popularity in Denmark and has been reprinted many times. The explanatory footnotes in the story are Goldschmidt's own.

The Battle of Marengo

In a small provincial Danish town a long time ago, it happened one morning that the Mayor, in leaving his house with the intention of walking diagonally to the other side of the street, had an accident which was so serious that it was very nearly a catastrophe. He had to go over a ditch—at that time there were not yet curbed gutters in the town, only ditches—and the board which extended from the door of the house across the ditch had that morning been pushed slightly to one side. As the Mayor, dressed in knee breeches of yellow leather, heavy woolen stockings held fast above the knees by formidable garters, and well-soled heavy shoes with buckles, not to mention the rest of his costume, which included a three-cornered hat and a peruke—as the Mayor, despite the insecure and tilting board, ventured across the ditch, he slipped, fell, and broke one leg. His screams quickly brought to the scene his wife, children, and servants, as well as his neighbors. The town's able barber-surgeon was fetched in great haste, as was his helper or apprentice, who also was an able man and, like his master, a German. True to their professional obligations and duties, they began to treat the leg very nearly in silence, with the seriousness and respect, and even kindness, which befits people who confront their superiors when the latter have suffered because of human frailties.

While this was happening, the patient's relatives and friends discussed the cause of the accident; an elderly maiden aunt held forth upon the subject of how many of the Mayor's forefathers had experienced the same accident—almost as if a broken leg were hereditary. A friend of the family, an elder citizen of the town, recalled earlier mayors who had broken a leg—as if what had happened was one with fees, emoluments, and other incidental sources of income. The entire town itself commiserated, partially out of sympathy for the Mayor, partially out of fear that the accident which had befallen him meant evil days for the city—as if it had been a comet. Only one person concerned himself with finding a tangible cause for what had happened; he was the town's policeman and professional public witness, sometimes also called the sheriff's boy. He looked for the evildoer—and found him in a shoemaker's boy who had lifted the board across the ditch outside the Mayor's door, and who for that reason was punished by flogging at the town hall. The Mayor listened to the case and let justice take its course, but some time later he admitted in strictest confidence to one of his closest friends that the reason he had broken his leg was that a button had been lost from his suspenders and that, when he wanted to straddle the ditch, he had been unable to take a long enough step and had therefore fallen. He had not commuted the flogging of the shoemaker's boy, for had the board not been touched, then he, the Mayor, would not have had to straddle the ditch, and would therefore not have had to expose himself to the dangerous results of having lost a button.

Although the man in whom the Mayor confided this was an honorable man and was used to keeping secret "what should be kept secret" (for he was a government official), the story nevertheless leaked out, simply because in any small town there is seldom a vessel without a vent—and from that moment, without a word having been said, the inhabitants of the town were divided into two parties, the Button party and the Board party. Yes, it can truly be said that from that day, no child was born in the town without being a Button child or a Board child from birth, and although the children were never instructed in animosity, they soon harbored resentments against one another, just as had the Guelphs and the Ghibellines, the Montagues and the Capulets, the Tories and the Whigs, and so on. The Button party was convinced that the button was innocent or as good as without blame and that the board and the boy were guilty. In addition to the sheriff's family and the town treasurer's family, the principal and masters of the Latin school et al. belonged to this party. The Board party, which was of the opinion that the button was to blame and that the board and the boy were without guilt, comprised the majority of common folk in the town. There is no doubt that both views might have been synthesized in a higher unity, to wit, in the belief that there had been something wrong with both the board and the button—as the Mayor himself had indeed remarked—but had anyone advanced such an opinion, he would have become a third party at loggerheads with the two others. Despite the fact that both parties were so fervent and firmly convinced, nevertheless, as aforementioned, the matter was never discussed aloud, and a stranger visiting the town for a short time would have left it praising the Mayor's fortunate regimen.

This was the situation until *Iversen's Journal* began to bring strange reports from Paris, first about Necker, then about Mirabeau and others, and finally about the whole upheaval which was called "revolution." In the beginning, the attitude of both the Button and the Board parties was one of unconscious or unexpressed pleasure, even at the storming of the Bastille. It was like observing a display of fireworks or a curious thunderstorm with distant bolts of lightning and subsequent fires. If either of the parties drew any conclusions and enjoyed a new and greater sense of importance from the course of events, it was at the club where the Button party met, and particularly among the schoolmasters. On the day when the mail arrived, the only day in the week when there were newspapers, members of the Board party met of an evening at the post office; they are remembered as being in good spirits, yet they were anxious about how long King Louis and his queen would tolerate such conditions. Mirth was engendered both at the club and at the post office when the newspaper reported the following: "A distinguished lady has died from pure indignation at the National Assembly's prohibition of livery and coats-of-arms. To see removed the only privilege which distinguishes people of quality and good family from bourgeois commoners is difficult indeed."

The state of mind in the town began to grow more tense and to show signs of a difference in opinion when this notice appeared in *Iversen's Journal*: "Some days ago in Valenciennes, where he is in command, the Duc de Noailles ordered that a young man who stumbled into him should be beaten. As a result, the citizenry put cockades on their hats and removed four cannon which stood in the marketplace; the army has joined them."

Soon thereafter the paper reported, "A smith has given to the National Assembly a gallows to hang aristocrats on. Wagon drivers call their horses aristocrats, and in restaurants a turkey is called an aristocrat. Also in Denmark there is a name for a turkey"—"Also in Denmark"!

It was Shrovetide and there was to be a celebration at which people were to try to "pull the neck off the goose." Rumor had it that a member of the Board party had said that a turkey ought to be substituted for the goose. Although it remained only a rumor, the sheriff nevertheless forbade that the celebration take place, on the grounds that it would be too cruel to the goose. Instead, the townspeople played "knock the cat out of the barrel."

Worst of all, a dark gloom spread over the town when the names of Robespierre and Marat started to appear in the newspaper. Then people began to read of dreadful happenings. As can be seen in the town archives, it was at this time that the shoemaker went to the district governor's office with a request that an inquiry be undertaken regarding the flogging which his son had received. When, as a result of an official communication from the governor's office to the sheriff, this was brought to the ears of the townspeople, the Button party was as surprised as it was indignant that such a scheme could be hatched in their town. People felt that things had gone as far as they had in Paris, and that the town had its own *canaille*; it was even said that there was a secret regicide club.

It cannot be denied that people were afraid. When the shoemaker walked up the street to the post office with the glazier and plumber on a Sunday, the entire Button party had the feeling that the town was on a shaky foundation, a feeling which was shared by the principal of the school, although he, besides being a good churchgoer, was at the same time, by virtue of his learning, a heathen—a stoic—and had as his motto Horace's *nil admirari*, "wonder at nothing."

It was also at this time that all documents pertaining to the flogging were sent by mail from the governor's office to the state chancellery.

If I had not already used the simile of thunder and lightning above, and if I were not ready to admit that the simile was inappropriate, then I would contend that the report that a young woman by the name of Charlotte Corday had stabbed Marat with a knife and caused his death came like a thunderclap. No, not like a thunderclap, except for the one party in the town; for the other party, it meant such delight and triumph over the shoemaker that one may safely say that many a town has since had a torchlight parade for less, although, to be sure, under conditions where rejoicing was shared more generally.

There was actually grief in the town among those who had grief enough already, the downtrodden and the poor; and the shoemaker's wife wept because of serious presentiments. And she was right, for a misfortune seldom comes alone, and it was not very long before *Iversen's Journal* reported that Robespierre had been declared an outlaw, had shot himself, shattering his lower jaw, and thereafter had been guillotined.

At the same time, the decision of the chancellery was received: a public announcement was to be made to the shoemaker at the town hall to the effect that, with regard to the flogging, he should cease and desist his protestation. One can imagine with what feelings the shoemaker and his son received the announcement at the town hall from the lips of the sheriff, who was surrounded by practically the entire Button party—while the Board party stayed at home almost to a man.

The Board party was crushed. At least it lay motionless, like a dog that has been beaten and starved into learning how to "play dead."

But after three years had passed, party spirit showed itself to be quite as immortal as in Dante's renowned Florence and raised its head again, although not in the same fashion as before. There was no longer a specific connection with the board across the ditch and the button, but the partisan division was exactly as before. A house which previously had been Button was still Button, and a house which had previously been Board was still Board. Nevertheless, there was at the same time a most remarkable peculiarity about the enmity between the parties as it now arose, for everyone, without exception, was completely of one mind and conviction about the same subject, and there was disagreement only about the proper transfer of authority. This sounds puzzling perhaps, but it becomes quite comprehensible when one discovers that the subject was the young French general Bonaparte, who had been in the public eye at Toulon, who quickly made his mark, and who had again been recognized at Arcole and elsewhere with enthusiasm. The only thing which was wrong with this enthusiasm and made it more restrained than boisterous in the town was that each of the parties wanted to have General Napoleon Bonaparte for itself and begrudged the other party his victories. This reflects a perhaps unusual but certainly deplorable aspect of human nature, which is not less significant if it remains unmentioned. In this case it determined the fate of the town.

It happened this way. General Bonaparte had become First Consul, and from the newspaper it was suddenly learned that the First Consul had quietly assembled an army at Dijon and had crossed the Alps. That in so doing he had imitated or even surpassed Hannibal was stressed with a display of considerable erudition in a lecture by the school's principal. The Board party, which did not know who Hannibal was and scarcely knew what the Alps were, nevertheless suspected something exceptional and great, and awaited the weekly mail with pounding hearts. It came, and with it the first report: General Melas had defeated the French. Both parties were assembled at the post office; each party thought the other welcome to the defeat but felt itself deserving of something better. While they were still standing there, together but nevertheless separated, in a heavy and apparently apathetic silence, a horseman was seen far down the highway and soon he was recognized to be a courier. He was a half-grown lad, who almost disappeared in the red jacket with a yellow collar that had been made for a grown man, and which hung on him as if he had put on an overcoat the summer day he was made a courier. Thrust out from the jacket's yellow neckpiece, as from an immense winged collar, was his face, which was reddish brown as a doughnut, for it was a warm June day. He was seen trying to blow his horn, but it would not obey him and gave forth only a few cracked sounds as he came rushing on in as fast a gallop as was possible for his old cart horse. As he rode toward the group of people, and before fulfilling his duty as a courier by delivering a letter or a handbill, he raised himself in his stirrups, removed his cap, and cried out with a voice hoarse with dust and emotion but nevertheless clear, "The First Consul was victorious at Marengo!"

A cry was about to arise from the assembled townsmen. They could almost have shouted and wept and thrown themselves in each other's arms. Both the Board party and the Button party looked upon one another and saw the well-known faces which had been repulsive and unpleasant from time immemorial. The one begrudged the other an outburst of joy—and there was silence.

From the moment that the shout of enthusiasm was stillborn, the town began to die. First, the school was closed; then the town itself lost its chartered privileges and became a mere village like Slangerup. But the boy who had been the courier grew up and became postmaster.

Maser: An Episode from Simon Levi's Life

Shortly after I had published *The Raven*, the editor of a periodical surprised me and at the same time did me a service by stating or suggesting that he had known Simon Levi—who, he said, was an upright and well-liked man—and as a result I wrote the editor in question the following letter.

> Dear Sir,
> In your esteemed periodical you described yourself as a personal acquaintance of a certain Mr. Simon Levi, to whom I had the occasion of referring in my story *The Raven*. Would you therefore have the kindness to permit me to inquire of you whether Mr. Simon Levi, in his personal association with you, told you anything in any detail about a certain Mr. Philpots and the peculiar circumstances that occurred for Mr. Levi and his sister, Miss Gidel Levi, after the said Mr. Philpots' death? If you have been in-

formed of these circumstances and you yourself have no need of them, would you be so kind as to relay to me such episodes and details as you might still remember and which serve our mutual friend's biography. If, on the other hand, they should be unfamiliar to you, might I perhaps dare to hope that after I have related them, you will nonetheless, in a note, tell your public that you knew of them in advance. It adds greatly to the worth of a story in the eyes of men of conscience, when a respected editor comes forward as a witness for the story's veracity.

Sincerely,
The author

I then received a reply that the editors indeed knew nothing at the moment of Mr. Philpots' death or of what occurred after his death, but that if something concerning this were publicly announced and they found the announcement plausible, the editors would take pleasure in attesting its truthfulness and actuality, since this is among the means by which editors make themselves interesting as well as useful.

This was for me a very agreeable letter, but I was surprised that the editor in question was not familiar with the fact to which I was most strongly alluding, since it was not the kind which is easily forgotten—Simon Levi had suddenly become very rich. The circumstances under which this occurred were in certain respects poetic, in others not; they are what I intend to relate.

Simon Levi was sitting in his humble little living room one Friday evening, enjoying, after the week's toil, the Sabbath's sanctity in the deepest peace. After the religious service, he had eaten a good soup and roast with his sister Gidel, then had said the prayer of thanks and sung a couple of David's psalms. Gidel had hummed along a little, until her brother's monotonous, subdued singing and her own humming had caused her to doze off. She was sitting with folded arms in a corner of the sofa and nodding, and the way in which she then half-awoke and hummed again for a moment some time after her brother had stopped singing showed that she reproached herself for not singing along. He had taken out a *Humash*—a Hebrew Bible—and had gradually become completely absorbed in reading. While he sat there, like this, with his old velvet *yarmulke* shoved back and a wisp of grizzled hair bristling out over his forehead, it was really not deep, gentle faith or piety that was reflected in his sharp, angular face, although there was obviously a religious mood present. But there was, in addition, a peculiar satisfaction, a subdued triumph, as if he were carrying on a trial and hearing his witnesses give all the evidence he wished. And it was indeed a trial: the six weekdays stood in his imagination summoned before the seventh day's judgment; but the six weekdays were accompanied by the whole of reality, and it was all reduced to nothing or to pure appearances and delusion in contrast to the great events and the great promises that concerned him and his race. He did not prove from any argumentation that the Bible was right; but the Bible as the only reality proved to him that all else was wrong. From time to time, without taking his eyes off the book, he reached out his hand and took a little of his dessert

—chick peas. But this was not that soup that is usually called chick peas. The peas were boiled in brine without their splitting, and were eaten cold, one at a time. As a great delicacy he now and then drank a little beer along with them. Scorn his taste, you Christian gourmets, but envy him his stomach.

When all is said and done, for such a man it can be a matter of indifference whether wealth or "luck," when it is abroad, steps into his house or not. But fate would not have it so; the great news came surprisingly, suddenly, and forcibly. Phillips or Philpots had died without heir in Buenos Aires and had willed his considerable fortune, after deduction of some grants, to be divided equally between Ferdinand Carøe, who had saved his life, and Simon Levi, who had once come to his aid with everything he owned. The Danish consul over there had submitted a report on the matter to the Ministry of Foreign Affairs, and one of its officials, a Counsellor of Legation, had himself undertaken to seek out Simon Levi to see how a man and a Jew looked when he suddenly became rich.

When there was a knock at the door, Levi assumed that it was the "Shabbas goy"—the Christian who for pay or out of friendship undertakes to trim the light and kindle the fire in the stove on the Sabbath, when one dare not touch fire—and after saying, "Come in!" and hearing the door open and close, without the wick of the light becoming shorter, Simon, who did not take his eyes off the book, uttered an impatient "Eh?" or rather "Eh-h?"

The visitor did not understand, but perhaps took pleasure in making the situation still a little more piquant, and therefore remained standing in silence, and so Simon Levi after a while added, "Eh! Why don't you trim the wick?"

The visitor found this amusing, took the snuffers, and trimmed the light.

"Now look after the stove," said Levi, still with his eyes on his *Humash.*

The Counsellor of Legation felt himself being drawn into a fairy tale like a Harun al-Rashid, and also condescended to the new service that was demanded; but the fire had gone out, and to build a fire was really too much for him. So he said, "The fire has gone out."

The voice seemed oddly unfamiliar to Levi, and he raised his eyes from his book. "What's this? Who are you? What do you want here? What business do you have here?"

"You asked me to feed the fire in the stove."

"Who are you? What do you want?" persisted Simon Levi, feeling quite uneasy.

"I have come to speak with the Commission Agent Levi."

"Yes, that's me," said Simon Levi.

"Yes, I presumed so. But I must also ask whether you can prove that you are Mr. Simon Levi."

"Prove? Who doubts it?"

"I don't doubt it. But can you establish that you are the Simon Levi who was born in Fredericia and learned the trade with a Mr. Heymann?"

"Establish it? Why should I establish it? My old employer doesn't owe me anything. He can lie peacefully in his grave, and this evening is my holy evening. Excuse me."

"But aren't you the one who knew a certain Mr. Phillips or Philpots?"

Now Levi realized that something was afoot, and it was as if the electric shock that went through him was imparted to his sister, who although she had awakened completely and stared at the visitor with all her might, still gave no sign of life or involvement, except for unfolding her arms as inconspicuously as possible.

"Phillips?" said Levi. "Do you come from South America? Please sit down."

"No, I am Counsellor of Legation Y–, and I come from the Ministry of Foreign Affairs."

Levi no longer asked with words; he *looked.*

The Counsellor of Legation continued, "Mr. Phillips or Philpots is dead."

"Dead?!" cried Levi. "Phillips dead! . . . Poor fellow! . . . *Boruch dayon emmes*![1] . . . What did he die of? . . . Um! Um! Phillips dead!"

"Yes, and has willed you two hundred thousand rix-dollars."

"Two hundred thousand rix-dollars? Me? Who are you?"

"I am Counsellor of Legation Y–."

"Can you prove that?"

"Here is my card," answered the Counsellor of Legation, smiling, "but you can, whatever day you wish, inquire at the ministry and obtain more detailed information."

"Am I dreaming?" said Simon Levi. "Gidel, did you hear that?"

1. Blessed be the righteous Judge!

"I don't know, Simon. I think so," replied Gidel gently.

"What did he say?"

"He said that Phillips had died and left you two hundred thousand rix-dollars."

"And you heard that he calls himself Counsellor of Legation and is sent from the Ministry of Foreign Affairs?" continued Levi with an almost threatening look at the visitor—a look that recorded his distinguishing features and seemed to want to hold him fast as a hostage.

The Counsellor of Legation said, "You will find everything as I have said, and I can add that you very likely have been cheated a little. In foreign countries they play fast and loose with such estates and permit as little as possible to slip away. But four hundred thousand rix-dollars is still a handsome sum to divide. I congratulate you. I wish you a good and peaceful night!"

When he had gone, Simon and Gidel stared at each other with an almost foolish look. They were outwardly passive because of inner agitation. It is much more poetic to imagine the arrival of such riches than to experience it. When one imagines it, the riches are not material, a heap of silver, gold, or banknotes, but the fulfillment of yearnings, the attainment of ideals, a great multitude of pictures of happiness, which show themselves on the threshold of existence, while the mind more or less distinctly sees in the background a strange figure of light, a spirit, a sprite, the goddess of fortune herself, with whom one feels oneself in mysterious kinship, and in whose presence one is, for a moment, as if transformed, idealized. If, on the other hand, wealth in reality comes, it indeed makes the great impression of surprise for a moment; but immediately afterward, in place of images of fantasy or beauty, there arise plans which engender restrictions, and perhaps anxiety. There is an almost physical effect in asking various parts of the body what pleasure they would have, and causing them at the same time to perceive their mortality. Like every sudden reality, it seldom fits completely into an accustomed routine; it seems as a rule to come too late; it is accompanied by a kind of pain, and in a case such as Levi's this pain is increased by the fact that the riches with all their reality nevertheless lack something—they are present only as a harbinger; the money is not in hand.

At last Simon Levi more or less regained his usual disposition and began to talk.

"Rich? Two hundred thousand rix-dollars . . . Gidel, can you understand that? Can you yourself feel that you are a rich girl—for you are! When I am rich, you're also rich—nonsense, you have borne half of my poverty. . . . Well, I won't say half. . . . But has any change taken place? We are rich people. . . . What is it to be rich? Gidel, my head is spinning. Can I eat more? I'm not hungry. Can I drink more? Can I stretch myself out to be six feet tall and become a soldier in the Royal Guard?—You shall have a black silk dress, Gidel. . . . But what if you do have a black silk dress? Sooner or later we will all be laid in our coffins, like poor Phillips.—Oh! Poor man!—We will be wrapped in a piece of linen and with a little earth under our head—what's money then? Can you take it with you? Nonsense, there must be something to it, a man from the Ministry of Foreign Affairs doesn't run around with idle chatter. . . . Two hundred thousand rix-dollars, two thousand times one hundred rix-dollar notes . . . eight thousand rix-dollars per year at four percent, and I should be a fool to get four percent—what would I do then?—Let's simply say five percent, that's ten thousand rix-dollars per year . . . ten thousand rix-dollars per year, Gidel! That's thirty rix-dollars per day. . . . But let me in *emmes*[2] have thirty rix-dollars per day!—What then? Thirty rix-dollars per day, what is that?—Gidel, I'll tell you something that we haven't talked about since we were very small children: my back is not straight like other people's. Nonsense, I have borne it now for so many years and never mentioned it before; but if I, for twenty-seven rix-dollars per day, could be rid of the little hump and keep three rix-dollars for sure and become a young man, or for three rix-dollars per day be rid of the hump and keep twenty-seven rix-dollars, then I would understand thirty rix-dollars per day! But what will I do now with thirty rix-dollars per day? The hump will remain, and the two hundred thousand rix-dollars maybe won't come, and it's better not to believe in it . . . although, nonsense, a man from the Ministry of Foreign Affairs cannot make fun of people.—Gidel, what good is it being rich when you don't have any money? Here we two rich people sit.—Can you tell by looking at me? Can I tell by looking at you, *nebbish*?[3] What does the Lord mean by that? Does He want to make fun of us two old people? Well, let's say He

2. Really.
3. Poor thing.

doesn't want to make fun of us, but that it is His will that we should not lack in our old days. Blessed be the Lord!—Gidel, I would wish that I could sleep tonight."

He made a movement as if to go into his bedroom, but stopped suddenly and said, "And what will my brother, that windbag, say?"

"He will be glad," said Gidel.

"Oh yes, he will be glad! And how will he be glad? He will immediately borrow four hundred thousand rix-dollars from me.—Gidel, I tell you, I command you: you must not say anything about the two hundred thousand rix-dollars."

"But Simon, do you think it can be hidden?"

"Hidden? Who says it's to be hidden, the fact that I have inherited a trifle? Didn't you yourself hear, he said that I had been cheated, I should have had much more? If they could have cheated me still more, they would have done it, you can swear an oath on it! Well, let the *schweilim*[4] in return do something to benefit me. Let us say—which heaven forbid, and I don't want to be taken at my word—but let us say they cheated me of one hundred eighty thousand rix-dollars, so I have twenty thousand rix-dollars left to tell my brother about, that windbag."

"He is too proud to come and ask you for anything, Simon," said Gidel; "but you've got to give *maser*, and you can just as well offer it to him as to a stranger."

"My brother proud! Oh yes, he's proud! Toward whom? Toward me, because I'm a poor man! And toward you, because you're a poor girl! But that doesn't matter! He has the right to be proud! He has to be the

4. Scoundrels.

head of the family! Aren't you sorry that he's not the one who's inheriting?"

"Simon, Simon, don't!" said Gidel, almost in tears. "Is that the blessing that wealth is bringing into the house?"

"What did I say, Gidel?—Nonsense, dry your eyes, your brother Simon is not going to hurt you. Don't say a bad word about the money. It's going to be a blessing yet; it will be a blessing, with God's help! You and I will be well off in our old days. Who knows, maybe you'll get a suitor. . . . Och, Gidelche, now I know why you want to have it known about the entire two hundred thousand rix-dollars: you want to gild yourself from top to toe, then they'll come running!"

Gidel laughed and said, "Oh yes, that was the reason!"

"How old are you, Gidel *lebe lang*?—Let me see, forty-seven. . . . In *emmes,* Gidelche, you *can* still get married; *I* will pay."

"Don't joke like that, Simon. Let me be an old maid and stay with you till I close my eyes for good."

"Gidel, you mustn't talk about that. You know, since I've begun to get older, I've often been struck by the thought, and it came again with all the money: What good is it all? All of us human beings will eventually be taken out and buried. Either I will die before you or you before me, and both ways are so discouraging, Gidel."

"Don't talk about it now, Simonche. We'll stay together, we two."

"Yes, if you don't go off and get married."

"Simon!"

"Now, now, I'll never say it again, unless you insist that people know about the entire two hundred thousand rix-dollars."

"If you don't want it, Simon, I won't talk."

"If you don't talk, I won't talk either. Let's go to bed now. Good night, Gidelche! See how a rich girl sleeps!"

It will now be necessary to say a few words about the brother Simon Levi had, and whom he for many reasons called "the windbag." In the first place, the brother was a big, handsome man who had adopted—in a superficial way, to be sure—the Christian spirit and mentality, and who associated with Christians in a completely different way from Simon. There was something in this casualness which Simon Levi had already, years before, called "windbagging." But in the second place, the brother, out of regard for his association with Christians, had Christianized or modernized his name a little. His name was really Mordocai, but since childhood he had been called "Mortche," and the most common translation of this is "Marcus." But since this also sounded rather strongly Jewish, Mortche had gradually toned it down to "Martin," which to Simon was a new instance of windbagging, though quite in harmony with everything else. "My brother, Mortche Martin," he was in the habit of calling him, but only to his sister Gidel; for Simon was still a poor man and did not criticize loudly. But when the occasion arose, he usually added, "When Mortche becomes Martin, then what does Simon become?" Then he could sit and make up all the names from "Søren" to "Sidse" and half-irritate himself, half-amuse himself over this, for what is a poor man to do? He must imitate the bee and strive to suck a little pleasure even from that which is bitter. This was, then, the second example of wind-bagging. The third and most important example was that Mortche or Martin was actually not well off, but still lived relatively grandly. He was just as optimistic as Simon was melancholy, and assumed that the Lord would certainly provide for him, if only he kept himself healthy and happy. "I will never be rich enough to leave my son and daughter anything," he was in the habit of saying, "so let them have a happy youth with my wife and me and learn to deal with people, and after my death they will do as I did after my late father's death—I got the bread I needed. What good is it being irritable and getting grey hairs on your head before one's time?" This, Simon Levi by nature could not forgive, especially since his brother, as a result of this philosophy, never had anything, or in any case only very little, left over for their sister Gidel, but let Simon provide for her alone. When his thoughts went in that direction, Simon would say to Gidel, "Your brother Mortche."

Of all the signs that Mortche or Martin lived too grandly, none was more unpleasant to Simon than that he had awnings in summer. Simon lived in a low ground-floor flat on the shady side, his brother in a third-floor flat on the sunny side, and Simon therefore felt that his brother could not be particularly plagued by the sun; but one thing Simon knew in any case, and that was that his parents and grandparents had not had awnings. The three white awnings outside his brother's windows were like flags for him, waving to attest an unnatural ambition, joy, or gaiety, and he could never go past without looking up and mumbling, "Awnings! Our *ovos ovoseinu*![5] Awnings!" But it was all a concealed mumbling; Simon was a poor man.

Meanwhile, Mortche's or Martin's children grew up, and he spoke of his son Frederik—in the synagogue at his birth, he had been named Shlomo for his grandfather, but "Shlomo" or "Salomo" can be literally translated "Frederik"—taking over the business, and at the same time there was some talk about Frederik's being in love with beautiful Rikke Jacobsen. Beautiful she was, and she also had the reputation for being a lively, good girl; but that was all, for Jacobsen could barely make ends meet. But this did not seem to worry Mortche or Martin; he said, "How much did I get with my wife?" It was not a full-fledged engagement, but the two young people were "talked about," and Simon Levi, since he also was acquainted with the young girl, could not help having feelings in this matter. He did not, however, express himself about it to a third party, but to Gidel he said, the first time the matter was brought up, "Wenn zwei Meisim tanzen, wer bezohlt die Kleisim?"[6]

His meaning was that since Frederik was handsome and clever, but not wealthy, he ought to try to make a good, that is, a wealthy match. But it is after all a question whether Simon Levi had this opinion except with his intellect; with his heart he could either wish the

5. Fathers' fathers.
6. "When two corpses dance, who pays the musicians?"

two young people good luck or, because he himself was overlooked, be pleased that his brother did not become attached to a richer family and thus be proved right with his windbagging.

This was the way matters stood at that extraordinary time when Simon Levi received the news of his large inheritance.

Simon did not sleep much that night. As soon as he had removed himself from the light which had shone on the visitor, and from Gidel, who had seen and heard him, the matter lost credibility; and he had to reestablish its credibility with the help of calculations of probability, or rather by contemplating the unlikelihood of anyone here being acquainted with Philpots and knowing anything about his youthful relationship to him, Levi, and making use of it for the sake of a cruel joke. But each time the matter in this way became probable, it again became too overwhelming really to be true, and a new anxiety appeared at the thought whether he had the right the next day—the Sabbath—to go to the Ministry of Foreign Affairs on a matter of business, in order to reassure himself. He proved to himself that such a sin really was not great, or at least was forgivable—and with that he dozed off; but when he awoke and got up, the doubts came back. In part he was alarmed at the thought of facing a man who would give him sudden, final, perhaps shattering certainty; in part he had a superstitious feeling that the wealth might disappear if he tempted God in the slightest manner and grasped for it on the very Sabbath.

When he came to the synagogue at the usual time and, unnoticed as usual, went to his seat in one of the farthest rows in the side aisle, he said to himself, "Oy, now it ought to be written on me in inch-high letters, 'Here comes a man worth two hundred thousand rix-dollars'—then we would see! What would we see? No, we wouldn't see! They would ask, 'Simon, where are the two hundred thousand rix-dollars?' " His neighbors, men in humble circumstances like himself, greeted him with the wish for a good Sabbath. Since the actual service had not begun, there was also a little time to ask each other how the week had gone. One shrugged jovially and said that you had to be content with what was bestowed on you. Another complained of the bad times. A third said that he had done an unexpectedly good piece of business the previous day, and had earned twenty rix-dollars. "In cash?" asked Simon Levi. "Yes." "Isch! That's more than I can say!" This ambiguity amused him; but he felt strange, like a prince whose lineage had been discovered and whose proofs of birth had been submitted to the king for decision, or like a bird whose wings had sprouted and which would soon start to fly, to the general amazement of those who had thought it a little, hunchbacked commission agent. As often happens with us when we quite fervently desire something for ourselves—the heart seems to swell with fervent love of God, who can give us what we wish for —so it was that Simon was religiously very moved and made grandiose but vague promises about the man he would become within the synagogue and the community. Then a man came in whom Simon knew to possess half a million. He was an impressive-looking, stout man, arrogant in appearance, but at the same time with an expression of seriousness and piety. He went to his seat near the prayer rostrum. A maiden who from the women's gallery sees her sweetheart come in could not have followed him with greater attention than that with which Simon Levi's sharp little eyes followed this man's every step. He was not received by anyone with slavish respect; no one bowed to him any more deeply than he to them; but nonetheless there was something in the familiar glance with which the more distinguished greeted him, in the esteem that seemed to hover in the atmosphere around the man, that told Simon Levi that esteem was not acquired with only two hundred thousand rix-dollars or more, but also with birth, family circumstances, the work of an entire lifetime. With sharp insight he perceived his own personal limitations and felt that in a certain respect wealth would cause him pain. Once more, and more definitely than the previous evening, he realized that no one must know the facts about the inheritance, that he would not seek wealth's trappings, but its reality, and then came a moment—but only a moment—when it became a matter of indifference to him.

Early the next morning he went to the factory near Elsinore and asked the Carøes if they had had any news. He wanted, it seemed, to approach any decision in as roundabout a way as possible. They answered that an inquiry had arrived; but since Ferdinand and his wife were away—Ferdinand had been given a ship to command—they knew nothing other than that Ferdinand had evidently received an inheritance from South America.

Levi breathed a deep sigh of relief. So here he was meeting the matter in the form of reality. He said, "I'm asking because I'm interested in the fact that Mr. Carøe is to become a rich man and because I'm also receiving a trifle on the same occasion."

"Aren't you going to share equally with Ferdinand?" he was asked.

"I am to have a share; but they are great scoundrels over there in South America, and I'm not getting more than twenty thousand rix-dollars. But that's good, too! I'm very well satisfied!"

The unsuspecting Carøes took that for the truth, and Levi felt certain that when the matter was reported from this source, it would be presented in the form he wished.

But he could not prevent the rumor from spreading quickly in Copenhagen, and not merely carrying the truth, but greatly exaggerating it. As an intelligent man, he then elected not to fight the current while it was strongest.

"Oh yes," he said, "I am inheriting a million. Will you give me nine hundred thousand rix-dollars for it?"

If anyone came and asked if it were not two hundred thousand rix-dollars, Levi would answer, "Are you making fun of me? Do you begrudge me more than two hundred thousand rix-dollars? It's three hundred thousand rix-dollars and stable and carriage house delivered free of charge. Do visit me when I get my carriage house."

He was shrewd, all right; but he was also dealing with sly people, who were not easily thrown off the scent, even though he tried to obliterate it. Several other things occurred, however, and made people doubtful. It was a long time before the money really arrived, so long that people were already smiling at the gold and silver mines that Simon Levi had in Peru and Mexico. When the money finally did come, it did not arrive all at once, but in installments, so that even well-informed people disputed the rumor about the large sums. And at that time there was not yet a sharp-eyed Assessment Commission in Copenhagen to prevent an honest man without a trade license from sitting quietly bent over his wealth without paying tax on it, or to publish his name in the "green book" of the city's most highly taxed citizens.

In this way Levi got his wish. But when all, or the greatest part, of the inheritance had finally been received, he was struck by a great inconsistency. He had suffered so much, from envy, from malice, from all the moods that arose with the shifting rumors. He had been torn from the stratum, the class of people to which he had hitherto belonged, if not through friendship, at least through that sort of comradeship that comes from shared circumstances. One moment he had become too rich for them, another moment he had been only a soap bubble reflecting the colors of wealth; then a kind of esteem had come again, the esteem that is always paid socially to a rich man, but this was not accompanied by friendship or sociability. He had acquired rank in a higher class, but only a titular rank; the person remained outside it, was and remained the little commission agent without culture and influence. Pained by this, he wanted to wave a magic wand and step forth in all his glory. On a holy day he had given five hundred rix-dollars to the poor. On that occasion he had been honored in the synagogue with a *mitzvah*; there was a ceremony carried out with the Torah. Since that sort of thing is arranged in advance with the same care as some court ceremony, he had been able to prepare himself for the day and make arrangements for a big banquet in his home. Only guests were wanting, but those he invited in the synagogue. He turned first, with dread and humility in his heart, to that impressive-looking rich man and asked him for the honor, and so forth. The impressive-looking man decided, since the invitation was given in the synagogue, to do a deed pleasing to God and be condescending; he answered with his deep guttural voice, "Why yes, why not? Just this once. I will come." Others said yes in a more well-bred way; still others excused themselves. Levi also invited a couple of poorer people, old acquaintances. One of them had watched closely to see whom he would invite first, and answered, "I am too plain for your new company. Birds of a feather flock together." There was for Simon a cruel irony in the last words, and contrary to habit, he could not come up with a single word in answer.

The party went to his home, and everything actually went very well, except for Simon. He could say over and over to himself, "I am a man with two hundred thousand rix-dollars," but he was not able personally to increase his stature and freely carry out a host's role. He knew that the host is indeed the humblest in his home, but also the first; that he must honor the most respected guest in the right way; and so on. But each time he, as host, wanted to approach the impressive-looking man, he felt himself to be in the shadow of a tower that rose over him, not only in the ratio of five hundred thousand to two hundred thousand, but in regard to the indescribable—many years' authority. Involuntarily, after several minutes he had found himself standing in a corner, in conversation with the poorest guest. He felt the falsity of his position and seized every opportunity to get out of the room and be away from it all. The aging brother and sister had a terrible moment in the bedroom. They were to go in to dinner, and Simon thought that Gidel should go in and choose the distinguished man as a table companion. Gidel would go in all right, but thought that the distinguished man must choose her.

"But what if he doesn't do it, Simon?"

"What if he doesn't do it?" said Simon, turning pale with dread and anger and unable to move.

"Simon *leb*," said Gidel finally, "they've got to go in to dinner. You go in and say to him, '*Seid moichel*'[7] and escort him to the table."

Simon answered after some hesitation, "I'll go in and say to him, '*Seid moichel*,' and if he won't be *moichel* to me—well! So I'll still be living tomorrow, if it is the will of the almighty God!"

At the dinner table, they naturally could not strike that social tone which arises from a community of intellectual interests. No matter how great a significance religion may have, neither in the church nor in the synagogue does one select his friends indiscriminately. But among Jews brought together by chance there is a common topic of conversation that can usually be turned to, and that is their interest in "Polish" stories. A peculiar naiveté blended with slyness, brazenness,

7. Excuse me.

pointed and sparkling wit, and self-irony seems especially to distinguish the Polish Jews, and anecdotes about them spread from the Leipzig Fair over all the lands where Jews understand the jargon, the blending of German and Hebrew which is called *mauscheln,* and which with its characteristic rhythm and its puns gives these stories their special spice. During the meal, which at first was silent and stiff, one guest began first to tell his neighbor such a story, then another remembered one that was also good, and a third had heard a new one. Soon they were as jolly as universal laughter can make a party. The impressive-looking man did not take over the conversation, but good-naturedly permitted the others to amuse him by telling the stories. Observing the happy turn of events, Simon Levi swam in ecstasy and began to think himself a real *balbos*, a great host. But fate would have it that it should take very little to topple him from his height. At a Christian dinner party where such funny stories were told, the high spirits would rise still further, lifted by the wine. But Jews drink very little. They are not easy to draw out of character, out of the overall sober-mindedness appropriate for practical people and for religious people who know that the meal must be ended with a dignified recitation of the long Hebrew prayer of thanks. They never entirely stop being a community, the religious stamp of which is blended with a national one. Therefore, it happened that the joviality evoked by the Polish stories changed into a certain warm, intimate discussion of Jewish conditions in general, of the fate of Jews here and in other countries. In one place there was persecution to talk about; in another place one or more Jews had risen high in society; Jews' mistakes were discussed, and as an example, one was named who somewhere had challenged the Christians with his wealth, always wanting to push himself forward, intriguing, showing off, but who had been humbled.

The impressive-looking man now took the floor and said, "Geschieht ihm recht! *Chutzpa!*[8] Served him quite right! One doesn't put on airs, even if one is a rich man. Money means a lot. Money is not everything."

The impressive-looking man was perhaps not thinking of Simon Levi at all when he said this, nor were the others, at first. But Simon immediately interpreted the words as an insinuation, and it was possibly the expression on his face that caused the others to hear the words again. The very nature of the conversation had led to a pause; now it became painful, and no one could bridge it. It was indicated that it was time to *bensche*—say the prayer of thanks—and with this Simon came out of the fit of paralysis that had seized him. But he forgot himself to the extent that, instead of inviting the worthiest or most distinguished guest to recite the prayer, he said it himself. While he, with all outward signs of devotion, with closed eyes and swaying upper body, recited the prayer, he realized his error, regretted it, but out of spite and anger was still in a way pleased with it, thought of his wealth, found it inadequate, was unhappy.

When the whole thing was over and the guests had left, Simon Levi, after a long silence, said to his sister, "Well, one time doesn't count! One time I have been

8. Insolence.

meschugge."[9] After another long silence, he added with that peculiar Jewish self-irony, "Listen, Gidel, do you know what? I don't understand it. It is said that happiness is a *nekeivo.*[10] Well, she is welcome! But what business does she have with me? I don't understand it. Why didn't she go instead to a young, handsome man? Can you explain it to me?"

Gidel answered, "Do you want to know that, Simon?"

"Do I want to know it! Why does one ask a question? Can you answer?"

"Because a young man would perhaps keep everything himself, but you can give to young men."

"Um!" said Simon, coming suddenly back into a line of thought that was not at all pleasant to him.

Long before he had the entire two hundred thousand rix-dollars under lock and key, right after the first installment, a painful question had arisen for Simon Levi. It was the question of *maser.* According to the Law, one must give one-tenth of whatever one acquires to the poor, and there are many more Jews than is believed who still today comply with this purely moral law. But when Simon Levi began to think about this duty and reflect on it, it seemed to him that there was a great difference between a man who had a regular income giving one-tenth of it annually, and one who suddenly received a large working capital. Should he, in accordance with the letter of the law, give one-tenth of the entire capital, that is, twenty thousand rix-dollars, or a tenth of the interest on the principal annually?

9. Crazy. But there is something comical in the word that is untranslatable.
10. Woman.

Seemingly, the result in each case would be the same, but his calculation was as follows: "If I give twenty thousand rix-dollars all at once, then I will have to give a further one-tenth of the interest on the remaining one hundred eighty thousand rix-dollars every year from now on, whereas if I keep the twenty thousand rix-dollars, then I can give the interest on it every year, and that can then be sufficient for the entire amount."

"Twenty thousand rix-dollars all at once!" added Simon to himself. "What upright Copenhagener will give twenty thousand rix-dollars all at once, because he's getting a little inheritance from South America? Who would be the first in line for it? My brother? Is he in need? Doesn't he have bread in the house? If he got twenty thousand rix-dollars, he would fly up and screech cock-a-doodle-doo like a rooster and walk all over me and be the first in the family, and then he would speculate with my money and ruin himself, that windbag!"

But the matter was by no means settled with this. Even granted that his assessment could stand as official vis-à-vis the Lord, or that he could rightfully regard himself as the responsible and taxable possessor of only twenty thousand rix-dollars and keep the rest entirely for himself, he had still invested the money in such a way that he earned five or six, sometimes seven percent on some of it, but only four percent on some. Which portions were the Lord's? The official interest rate was four percent.

At last the matter became utterly tangled by a final circumstance. We have seen that Levi gave five hundred rix-dollars to the poor on a holy day. He had previously given his brother Mortche or Martin a thousand rix-dollars, and thereby thought he had done a good piece of business. His brother had come to him, and with the casualness, intimacy, or condescension that Simon could not resist, he had induced Simon to talk and to admit, though in indefinite terms, that the inheritance was quite a good sum of money. Then his brother had, as if in passing, hinted at a note for a thousand rix-dollars which he had to pay, and Simon, in order not to forfeit a larger sum for his imprudent remarks, had at once said to his brother, "Let it be *maser*." And then his brother had accepted it, seemingly heartily satisfied, but convinced that there was much, much more that Simon owed him before God.

So this amounted to fifteen hundred rix-dollars, and in addition Simon had quietly given here and there some few sums to the amount of a couple of hundred rix-dollars, which he scarcely had the heart to credit to the Lord's account, since this charity had occasioned happiness for himself; but he nevertheless entered them in the books. In all, approximately seventeen hundred rix-dollars.

If one now has the patience to make an arithmetical calculation, one will see that—accepting Levi's official assessment of the inheritance at twenty thousand rix-dollars as correct—his yearly income from the inheritance, according to the four percent interest rate, was eight hundred rix-dollars; according to this calculation, he thus before the Lord had a credit of not less than nine hundred rix-dollars.

Even if the interest on the twenty thousand rix-dollars were set as absurdly high as seven percent—to the amount of fourteen hundred rix-dollars—he would have a credit of three hundred rix-dollars.

And the only unpleasant aspect of this favorable balance sheet was that it was only nominal, that conscience could make a different calculation, and that it had no other excuse than the fact that since he did not have the enjoyment of the entire wealth, he ought not to have to pay the whole tax on it. But there is perhaps many an honored fellow citizen who in filling out his income tax return ends in a similar dilemma when faced with the question of what is capital and what is income, how high he feels he should be taxed, and how high the Assessment Commission would think they could set him.

The anxiety involved in keeping two different accounts which absolutely would not balance stayed in Levi's mind and caused him at times to do things that people could not understand. For instance, he once attended an art auction, not to buy anything, but to be among the right sort of people and have a chat, since he was now so often bored. There was an art connoisseur or art lover present who, happening to meet Levi and observe him, did not credit him with enthusiasm for art, but assumed that he was a buyer. He told Levi that some of the paintings especially merited attention; that the artist was dead, had during his lifetime struggled against neglect and poverty, and that only now was his talent recognized. Levi bought over a thousand rix-dollars worth at one time, which was partly because he suddenly felt himself reminded of *maser* and saw in artists some of the poor to whom he, strictly speaking, owed money, but partly because he also wanted to let the Christians see that an appeal to a Jew was not made in vain, and, finally, he had so many empty walls at home. Immediately thereafter he was plagued by the uncertainty about which account should be credited with the thousand rix-dollars. Were they a new advance payment to the Lord, or an installment on the debt, or neither, since he himself had, after all, received the paintings? But, as he quite correctly said to himself, would he ever, for his own sake, have permitted himself the luxury of buying paintings? Wouldn't he have been content with copperplates or lithographs? On whose account, then, should the thousand rix-dollars be entered?

His intellect, which knew the law all too well, gave the answer extremely clearly and unpleasantly; his spirit wrapped itself in darkness and found a hiding place, but was never able to hide.

If a person should constantly think about his transgression or his dealings with the Lord, he would have either to bring the matter to complete atonement or to lose his mind. Merciful nature, which has made us frail, has also to a certain extent given us a remedy against frailty's fear—we are able to think of other things. And, as a result of the art purchase itself, Simon Levi had for a time other things to think about. That purchase drew people's attention once more to him and his wealth, and they came to the conclusion that he was very rich, but did not understand how to handle money. In short, they thought that he had a *schrull.*[11] This resulted in a man approaching him with a proposal.

11. A word the meaning of which lies approximately halfway between an overwrought state and having a screw loose.

There was a very distinguished, but also very much indebted, person in a foreign country who wanted to float a loan and mortgage his property, only a sixth or seventh mortgage to be sure, but the reigning prince, his relative, who did not exactly want to guarantee the loan, was nevertheless interested in it and promised he would knight the lender. In spite of all Simon Levi's good sense, a fire was kindled in his spirit at this temptation. His wealth had, up to now, given him such little satisfaction, so little of both external esteem and internal peace. Even in his own family he was not sure of being first; his big, jovial brother, who accepted his money, needed only to show himself in order to tower over him. But if he were granted an order of knighthood! If it were printed in the newspapers that *Rentier* S. Levi was most graciously named knight of such and such an order! Those who knew him would ask just what he had done. "Well, let them ask! People also get tired of asking when they don't get an answer. Let them pick away at it. After a while, the decoration will be quite secure anyway, and will be like any other form of recognition. And on *Shabbas* when I come from the *schul*[12] with Gidel on my arm, and we go up Nørregade to the old city wall, past the fire guard, then the fire guard will have to present arms, and if we go around to Amalienborg, then the royal guard with their tall hats will have to present arms. No question about it! They must! What a *s'khie*[13] for Gidel, poor girl, to live to see it! And if I visit my brother . . . nonsense, if it had been printed in the newspapers, he has to respect

12. Synagogue.
13. Joyous privilege.

it, and if he thinks anything, then I'll think something too, and will say to myself, 'When you're a *kotzin,*[14] you can buy an order of knighthood.—What are you going to do about it?' "

It did not, however, escape Simon Levi's attention that when a simple commission agent approached him in such a matter, there must be something not quite above suspicion about it, in a financial respect. It was clear to him that he would lose money; he merely wanted to see clearly and know how much real security there was and how much would be lost. When the negotiations began, no firm commitment was made, probably because there was absolutely nothing solid there, and then a new, unexpected difficulty appeared. When precise information was received at the place in question as to who was to have the order, they became uneasy. The circumstances were such that at the moment they did not want to make fools of themselves by decorating a man who, indeed, as it appeared, was honest and of unblemished reputation, but was a little Jew in one of the side streets, not even a stockbroker, let alone a banker. But Levi learned nothing of this. They put him off in order, perhaps, if everything else failed, to make use of him. The distinguished person in question even wrote him several condescending letters, in which he hinted how nice it would be if he, Levi, *first* performed his service, and *then* waited for the reward. But that stupid, Simon Levi was not.

While Levi was occupied with this fata morgana, he also made his peace with his conscience. He decided to

14. Rich man.

establish a fund—after his death there would be established a foundation for old maids which would bear the name "Sir S. Levi's and his Sister Gidel Levi's Foundation." Once each year there would be held a special religious service in which his name would be commemorated and a song sung. In his thoughts he enjoyed the ceremony as if he were present at it. With regard to his balance sheet, he said to himself, "Do I go on binges? Do I drink? Do I gamble? Do I want to squander the money the Lord has sent me? So little will I squander it, that on the contrary it will increase! Where could He, with all due respect, have gotten a better administrator than me, even if I too must have my own free will a little?"

This was a happy time for Levi; but like all happiness that is too much grounded on fantasy, it was not to be long-lived, and the blows that came did not come from one side alone.

Storm clouds had gathered close by. Now, Simon's brother Mortche or Martin was of an optimistic nature, and the thousand rix-dollars he had received, plus the assurance of considerably more that for the moment was being withheld from him, induced him to speculate. Instead of turning over the business to his son and letting him get married, he himself set to work with renewed zeal "so that son and daughter-in-law would come into something considerable." Once one is committed to this course of action, the plan is very simple: one buys on credit in large lots, and one procures a relatively large profit for onself by selling on credit in smaller lots, and as long as one's outstanding accounts are properly paid in, there is a real profit.

Circumstances were favorable for Mortche; people gave him credit, partly because he was well liked, partly because it was assumed, both here and in Hamburg, that his brother was backing him. And for a time his outstanding accounts were paid in as promptly as clockwork; he paid his creditors, was given new credit, expanded. He had become a member of the society of wholesale dealers. Now his son was to be his partner, an official offer of marriage was made at the Jacobsens', and the wedding was set for the autumn. Then there was great festivity in the two families. Simon Levi saw that his brother threatened more and more to become "the first in the family," but submitted to this and participated with quiet dignity in the festivities; his eye was fixed on the decoration to come.

But suddenly a Hamburg firm went bankrupt, and with it fell one of the pillars of the large but fragile edifice which Mortche Levi had hastily erected. The danger lay not simply in the fact that money was owed this firm, but also—and chiefly—in that it had been involved with a large number of merchants in the provinces, debtors of the firm of "M. Levi." How many of them would remain solvent? Here and there it was apparent that the money could be salvaged by treating the merchants in question leniently or even by helping them over the crisis. In short, the firm of Mortche Levi needed money and more money.

Who was closer at hand than Simon? Mortche went immediately to him, too, but at a most unfortunate time; for Simon had just learned that the distinguished person had solved his problem in some other way—the radiant decoration had disappeared from the horizon.

He was sitting in the dark, as if sunk in a deep well, and he felt himself so pitiably small, angry at fate, angry at himself because he had hoped, believed, and been a *behaima*.[15]

Mortche saw a gloomy face, but assumed that Simon knew what had happened, and he was himself long since accustomed to the fact that a man who is to pay out money is like ice and must be gently thawed out. In this case, however, he assumed that great efforts would not be needed. He had not lost the proud feeling of being a wholesaler. He felt convinced that his "house" actually was stable and his business "handsome"; what was needed was not a gift but a loan that could help him out of a momentary embarrassment and lift him even higher than before. He had no idea that this was the greatest sacrifice he could, at the moment, demand of his brother—Simon was supposed to lift him and thereby push himself down still lower! Simon was supposed to give up all hope for himself, and only make his brother great!

So Mortche presented the matter in a wholly businesslike way, demonstrated the nature of the embarrassment, and demanded of his brother not a definite sum, but a promise to help according to circumstances, in return for the usual guarantee and the usual interest rate.

After a pause, Simon said, "Now listen, Mortche, I must tell you this, you are no solid merchant."

"What else is new?" Mortche answered, forcing himself to laugh. "Where should solidity come from? What

15. Been a fool, let himself be deceived.

our late father left, God and everybody knows, and I have received no other inheritance."

"It's not that," continued Simon. "It's not that you are a *dalfen;*[16] many a man begins with nothing; but he waits to spread out until he has something. When you were a little man, you had to have three big awnings; and when you got a little in your hands, you had to give credit from here to Ringkøbing and from Skagen to Neumünster—to make people open their eyes wide over the whole country. Isch!"

"Well," answered his brother, "when it is heaven's will for things to go wrong for a man, he has to have it thrown in his teeth. I have done my best, but maybe I have made mistakes. I have made mistakes. *Oshamti, bogadti. . . .*[17] Shall I recite the whole thing, Simon?"

"You will not recite the whole thing. Who am I? A sinner before God. You will only grant me that you are no solid merchant."

"I said that. But now I'll say one more thing, Simon! I have believed that you were a good person."

"When someone gives away his last shilling, then he is a good person."

"That's not the point. You can give or not give—although who is talking about giving? You can lend or not lend. But you don't dare to reproach your brother for something when the Lord has touched him."

"I'm not reproaching! I'm not saying anything but what I can defend before God: you are no solid merchant. And why do I say that? To reproach you for it? God forbid! How can you help it? That's the way you

16. A poor man.

17. First words of the great Jewish confession of sins.

are. But when you yourself come and say that I must help you, then I say, Mortche, I know you. What is on the debit side you see as rosy red, and what is on the credit side you see as lily white. That is your nature; I'm not reproaching you for it. I reproach? But when I'm to invest my little bit of money in your business, then I won't rely on your figures—not because you will deceive me, but because you *see* in your own way—and therefore, I say let a couple of businessmen, real businessmen, audit your accounts, let everything be clear and light as day, and then we will see."

Mortche could not deny to himself that there was some fairness in this, although he naturally would have by far preferred that the matter pass off quietly and that no outsider have access to his books. Now too, he had a feeling that even if Simon's provisional condition were fulfilled, the matter would not go completely smoothly. But there was nothing else he could do. To seek help from others and thereby proclaim that his own brother considered his position hopeless would immediately plunge him into ruin.

Before he left the house, however, he wanted to secure an ally to plead his case while he was away. He went in to see his sister and told her that his firm was in danger. Gidel had been ailing for some time, and on that day she was very ill and nervous. She burst into loud weeping.

This strong sympathy broke Simon's heart as an ingratitude and a slight toward him. He could not understand her affection or apparent partiality for his brother, and she probably could not understand it herself. She loved Simon without thinking about it, without having her love measured or put to the test. He was in a way her second self. She loved Mortche not "because," but "notwithstanding," in spite of what Simon called his windbagging, but also because he was married and had children, and finally because Mortche had something in his nature that brought pleasure, a breath from a more lively realm, a flash of poetry. And now the world was about to crush this, the only poetic blossom she knew.

Simon submitted to the slight, or his displeasure with her was soon over, but he would not be swayed; he stood behind a strong redout. To her best arguments he answered, "When a man brings me a sack without a bottom and demands that I fill it, I answer, 'Have a bottom sewed in your sack, my good man, and then come back.' And that's that!"

A short time later Mortche brought the audit that Simon had demanded. It was signed by two reliable men and said in effect that the firm of M. Levi under the present circumstances required twenty thousand rix-dollars.

Simon cried out as if in bodily pain. The sum seemed too large to him, and its size bore a sinister likeness to that sum he should have paid in *maser*, but on which he was only paying the interest. He had actually paid more than the interest; to the sums we are already acquainted with, he had gradually added not insignificantly in philanthropical donations. According to the double or ambiguous bookkeeping which he had preferred and become accustomed to, he had a considerable credit before the Lord, and, nevertheless, the entire sum was now being demanded—*maser* for the entire two hundred thousand rix-dollars. In this there was something strangely taunting that provoked him to resistance. The whole thing seemed to him to be a conspiracy in which people were laughing quietly up their sleeves and trying to make him his brother's footstool. There was something peculiar in this—not exactly unjust, but crafty—that caused the spitefulness to rise within him; he would not do good under that compulsion and in that way.

Although he had already made his decision, he nevertheless read through the papers with seemingly great attention and finally said, "That's clear and bright as day! Twenty thousand rix-dollars to your creditors!"

"Yes," said Mortche, "but then there are prospects that all the outstanding accounts will be paid in."

"Prospects? Oh yes, prospects. Remote prospects. And if they are not paid in? And if the firm of M. Levi in the meantime speculates and comes up with a deficit again? No, Mortche, you are my brother, and whatever service I can do for *you*, I will do for you, but I won't pay your creditors."

"But Simon, then I'll go bankrupt!"

"So you'll go bankrupt. Larger firms have been seen to go bankrupt."

In vain his brother emphasized what a humiliation it would be for the whole family if he went bankrupt, in vain he suggested that his son's wedding would probably be called off. Simon had said what he had to say, and to his "no" he merely added, "Because you make debts, I'm supposed to pay! Because there's to be a ball, they're going to dance on top of my head! Oh, *nit*! Let everything be swept clean! They probably won't run off with Rikke Jacobsen in the meantime, and if I have a little, there will also be a little for your Frederik."

"That means," cried his brother, "you will have *rachmones*[18] and give us alms! I'll come to you and get a weekly allowance from the *maser* you have to pay! No, Simon, not yet! I'll sell everything first—my little bit of silver, the comforter from my bed—I'll do anything! You're leaving me in the lurch.—God will help!"

Cold sweat stood out on Simon's forehead as his brother, with these words, went out the door, but the good in him did not have the power to call him back. He did not *want* to pay Mortche's creditors, he *wanted* to see him go bankrupt, he *wanted* to be the first in the family himself and then help according to his own "free will."

In spite of those strong words, Mortche still did not think that the matter was terminated; he was relying on his sister. But Gidel's indisposition had worsened; the pain made her apathetic; and, in a way that Mortche could not anticipate, she became an instrument against him. Sympathy and anxiety for Gidel formed a new and secret excuse for Simon with regard to his brother —when he looked after her so completely as he did, he could turn his face away from more questionable duties.

But it was written in the book of fate that precisely where Simon wanted to forget, he was to be reminded in an unusual way.

Nothing was spared on Gidel; she had not only one of the city's most celebrated doctors, but also the best

18. Compassion.

Jewish nurses; straw was laid in the street in front of the house so that she would be able to sleep. Every time Simon came out on the street, he regretted that Gidel herself could not see that in her sickness she was being treated like a princess. In the silence which the carriages suddenly observed near the house, there was something almost as solemn as in prayer in the synagogue. But her illness grew worse or approached a crisis, and the doctor declared that he would have to resort to an operation.

"Is there any danger involved?" asked Simon anxiously.

The doctor answered, "We are all in God's hand; but I don't see any real, imminent danger. It should not be put off; I will come a little after noon."

When he had come back with his instruments and had arranged them, Simon Levi's sharp eyes noted that he made the sign of the cross over them. Although one seldom in one's daily life sees this sign made, Levi was acquainted with it almost by instinct and assumed that the doctor was worried about the outcome of the operation. He said with pursed lips, which made him look both ingratiating and a little malicious, "Excuse me, Professor, you made a little cross over your knives. Would you be angry if I asked, what does that mean?"

The professor was almost embarrassed; people in his profession do not customarily flaunt piety, and certainly do not come into conflict with the religious feelings of others. He answered softly and almost apologetically, "You must not be afraid or get angry, Mr. Levi, sir. It is merely a sign that I usually make, in my

God's name, when another person's health and perhaps life are in my hands."

"Oh, a sign . . . in your God's name . . . Professor," said Simon in a tone that sounded to the doctor like stupid courtesy. "Would you wait a moment, Professor? Would you be so kind as to wait a moment?" he added immediately and went into his sitting room.

He began to pace up and down agitatedly, as if he were looking for a place to hide, while he said to himself, "*Was is do mehr?* What's wrong? Simon, don't be a fool! There's nothing wrong. He is a capable man. Nonsense, I can rest easy, I've done my duty. So he made a sign! What's a sign? It's easy to make a sign; that doesn't cost anything! If the sick can be cured by making signs, then there won't be many apothecaries. And what concern of mine is it? The sign does not *shmatte*[19].—But I didn't like it when I saw it.—I *don't* like it; it makes me uneasy, I am uneasy . . . . It was as though there were another person in the room. And who is it? He says it is his God. *Kemekh!*[20] If it is the real God, it is after all my God.—*Adonai Eloheinu,*[21] if it was You and You were watching them pulling and tearing and cutting on my sister Gidel in order to make her healthy, and *Bal hamoves*[22] was standing outside, and You then said, 'Why doesn't her brother Simon pay me the money he owes me?' . . . *Shema Yisroel,*[23] I

19. Baptize.
20. Unintelligent person, fool.
21. Our Lord, our God!
22. The angel of death.
23. "Hear, O Israel!" The Jews' great invocation and cry of fear.

can't stand it, my head is spinning? . . . How much do I owe Him? . . . Nonsense about that foundation after my death! If He wants His money and will cure Gidel, I have to pay while I'm still alive.—How much is it?"

He opened a drawer, took out some papers, and began to calculate with great care, completely mechanically to be sure; for he well knew the sum, and the question was merely one of reaching a decision.

The doctor opened the door, saw with wonderment or amazement Simon Levi even at such a moment sitting with his papers and calculating, and said, "Excuse me, Mr. Levi, sir, but I can't very well wait for you, especially if you have many important transactions."

"Important transactions? It *is* an important transaction! More important than you think! I'm coming now."

He screwed his eyes and almost his whole face together and said, "Now it's done."

Then he went in to see his sister and said, "Gidel, my sister *leb*, let him proceed, in the Lord's, the almighty God's name. I tell you, you're going to get well."

"How can you say that so confidently?" said Gidel gently, shaking with fear as she prepared herself.

"How can I say it? Listen, Gidelche, put your head up here, like this . . ."

And whispering into her ear, Simon Levi said, "I have paid *maser*. Your brother Mortche will have the twenty thousand rix-dollars; he will be first. I owe it to our Lord—He will be present—although not that much, but He shall have it, all twenty thousand, for your sake. Now you don't need to be afraid, Gidelche, and I'm not afraid either."

"Simon," said Gidel, "*Gott soll Dir benschen!* God will bless you!"

From that time on, Simon Levi was much happier than before; he had peace of mind, was in his own way cheerful and playful in his daily life, gentle and benevolent, so that he acquired that good name which, as already mentioned at the beginning of this narrative, was accorded him. He also acquired prestige, although not in a large circle. When his brother's affairs were put in order and the business was again going well and more solidly than before, his brother's son Frederik was married to Rikke Jacobsen. It was a big wedding, and when Simon saw the bride in the white veil under the *chuppa*,[24] and his nephew merrily smash the glass under his foot, and his sister and the people around dressed up and solemn, and he thought that this beautiful sight was in no small part his work, he closed his eyes and said, "I thank You, almighty God, for taking the twenty thousand rix-dollars from me, and You will in the future receive everything honestly and more to boot!"

At the table toasts were proposed, first to the bride and bridegroom, then to the bride's parents; but then when the person whose turn it was rose to propose a toast to the bridegroom's parents, Mortche interrupted him politely and said, "First we must have another

24. The canopy under which the wedding takes place.

toast to drink. My brother Simon goes first. Why should we deny what everybody knows? This is his work. My grandchildren's children will bless his name. For this we can all give three cheers."

When Simon began to recover from his emotion, he felt something soft around his neck and something warm at his cheek. It was the bride.

May it go thus for those who themselves have no children!

Jens Peter Jacobsen

"Mogens" was first published in the periodical *Nyt dansk Maanedsskrift* 3 (1871–72): 439–61, 489–507. It was included in the volume *Mogens og andre Noveller* in 1882 (reprinted several times) and in 1888 appeared in an often-reprinted volume of Jacobsen's collected works.

Mogens

It was summer, the middle of the day, in a corner of the enclosure. Straight ahead stood an old oak tree; one might say that its trunk was writhing in despair at the lack of harmony between its quite new yellowish foliage and its great, black, gnarled branches, which resembled most of all crudely distorted ancient Gothic arabesques. Behind the oak was a luxuriant hazel thicket with dark, lusterless foliage so dense that neither trunks nor branches were visible. Above the hazel thicket rose two straight, joyous maple trees with gaily serrated leaves, red stems, and long tassels of green seed clusters. Behind the maples the woods began—a green, symmetrically rounded slope where birds went in and out like elves in a grassy hillock.

All this could be seen when one walked along the path outside the fence. If, however, you were lying in the shade of the oak with your back against the trunk and looking in the other direction—and there was someone who was doing just that—then you first saw your legs, then a little spot with short, lush grass, next a large clump of dark nettles, then the hawthorn hedge, the large white convolvuluses, the stile, a bit of the rye field on the other side of the fence, the counselor's flagpole over there on the knoll, and then, finally, the sky.

It was oppressively hot; the air quivered from the heat, and it was so quiet; the leaves hung drowsily on the trees; there was nothing moving except the lady-bugs on the nettles and some dried leaves lying in the grass, which curled up with small sudden movements as if they were shrinking under the sun's rays.

And now the person under the oak: he was lying and panting and looking disconsolately, helplessly, at the sky. He hummed a bit, gave it up, whistled, gave that up too, turned over, turned over again, and let his eyes rest on an old molehill which had turned a light gray because of the dryness. Suddenly a little round dark spot appeared on the light gray dirt, another, three, four, many, still more; the entire mound was quite dark gray. The air was nothing but long, dark streaks; the leaves nodded and swayed; and there came a rushing sound that turned into a seething; the rain poured down.

Everything glimmered, sparkled, sputtered. Leaves, branches, tree trunks, everything glistened with moisture; every little drop which fell on the earth, on the grass, on the stile, on anything at all, splintered and sprayed into a thousand tiny pearls. Little drops hung a moment here and became large drops, dripped down there, joined other drops, became little streams, disappeared into little furrows, flowed into large depressions and out of small ones, sailed away with dust, with splinters and bits of foliage, stranded them, set them afloat, spun them around, and stranded them again. Leaves which had not been together since they were in the bud were reunited by the water; moss which had withered away in the dryness suddenly revived and became soft, woolly, green, and spongy; and gray lichens which had almost turned to snuff spread out in neat frills, stiffening like brocade, and with a sheen like silk. The convolvuluses let their white corollas be filled to the brim, toasted each other, and poured the water over the heads of the nettles. The fat black slugs inched amiably along and looked up appreciatively at the sky. And the man? He was standing bareheaded in the rain, letting the raindrops beat down on his hair and brows, eyes, nose, and mouth, snapping his fingers at the rain, lifting his feet slightly from time to time as if he were going to dance, shaking his head now and then when there was too much water in his hair, and singing at the top of his voice, without any idea of what he was singing, because he was so preoccupied with the rain:

"If I had, O if I had a grandson, yes,
And a chest with much, much gold
Then I would have had me a daughter, yes,
And a house and a home and a field and a fold.

If I had, O if I had a daughter, yes,
And a house and a home and a field and a fold,
Then I would have had me a true love, yes,
with chests with much, much gold."

As he stood there and sang, over between the dark hazel bushes a girlish head peeked out. Some fringe from a red silk shawl had caught on a branch which protruded somewhat farther than the others, and from time to time a little hand reached out and tugged at the fringe, but this only led to a little shower from the branch and its neighbors. The rest of the shawl was stretched taut over the girlish head, and hid half her forehead, shaded her eyes, then suddenly twisted away and was lost among the leaves, but reappeared gathered in a large rosette of folds under her chin. The girlish face looked very astonished but was just about to laugh; the smile was already in her eyes. Suddenly the person who was standing and singing in the rain took a few steps to one side, saw the red fringe, the face, the big brown eyes, the astonished little open mouth; instantly he became self-conscious; astonished, he glanced down at his clothes, but at the same instant there was a little cry, the protruding branch swayed violently, the red fringe disappeared in a flash, the girlish face was gone, and there was a rustling farther and farther away on the other side of the hazel bushes. Then he ran. He did not know why; he did not think at all; the merriment evoked by the rain welled up in him again, and he ran after the girlish face. It did not occur to him that it was a person he was running after; it was *only* the girlish face. He ran; there was a rustling on the right, a rustling on the left, a rustling in front, a rustling in back; he rustled, she rustled, and all this noise and the running itself made him eager, and he called out, "Say peekaboo, wherever you are." Nobody said peekaboo. Hearing himself shout, he became a little uneasy, but he kept on running; then he was struck by a thought, but only a single thought, and he murmured while he continued to run, "What are you going to say to her? What are you going to say to her?" He approached a large bush; she had hidden *there*; he saw a bit of her dress. "What are you going to say to her? What are you going to say to her?" he continued to murmur all the while he was running. He reached the bush; turned quickly aside; ran on, murmuring the same thing; came out onto a wide path; ran a little way down it; stopped suddenly and broke into laughter; walked, quietly smiling, a little way farther; and then laughed with all his might and continued doing so across the entire clearing.

And then it was a beautiful autumn day; the way down to the lake was completely covered by the lemon yellow elm and maple leaves, and here and there were also blotches of darker foliage. It was so pleasant to walk on this tigerskin rug and observe how the leaves snowed down and how the birch looked still more delicate and graceful with so little on the branches and how the mountain ash looked magnificent with its heavy red clusters of berries. And the sky was so blue, so blue, and the woods seemed much larger; one could see such a long way between the tree trunks. And then too all this would soon be over; woods, field, sky, and open air would have to make way for the time of lamps, rugs, and potted hyacinths. And for this reason the counselor from "Cape Trafalgar" and his daughter were walking down to the lake, having left their carriage at the county official's.

The counselor was a friend of nature. Nature was something quite special; nature was one of the most exquisite ornaments of existence. The counselor championed nature; he defended it against the artificial. Gardens were nothing but nature corrupted, but formalized gardens were nature deranged; there was no formality in nature; the Lord had wisely made nature natural, nothing but natural. Nature was what was unbound, uncorrupted; but with the Fall, civilization had overtaken mankind; now civilization had become a necessity, but it would have been better if it had not been so; the natural state was something quite different, quite something else. The counselor would have nothing against sustaining himself by going around in a lamb's skin and shooting rabbits and snipe and plover and grouse and wild boar. No, the natural state was indeed a pearl, a real pearl.–

The counselor and his daughter walked down toward the lake. It had long been sparkling through the branches, but now, when they turned the corner where the large poplar stood, it came into full view. *There* it was, with large shards of glassy water and jagged tongues of blue gray rippled water, with strips that were bright and strips that were rippled, and the sunlight rested motionless on the bright ones and flickered on the rippled ones. It drew the eye across its surface, led the eye along the shore in gradually rounded arcs, in abruptly broken lines, swung the eye around the green tongues of land, then released it and disappeared in large bays, but carried the thought with it.–To go sailing! Were there boats for rent?

No, there were not, said a little boy who lived in the white farmhouse and was down on the shore skipping rocks across the water. Were there no boats at all? Oh yes, there were boats all right. There was the miller's, but that couldn't be had; the miller wouldn't allow it; the miller's boy Niels had nearly got a beating when he lent it out the last time; there was no good even thinking of it; but there was the gentleman who lived up at Nikolai the gamekeeper's; he had an excellent boat, black above, with a red bottom, and he lent it to anybody and everybody.

The counselor and his daughter went up toward Nikolai the gamekeeper's. Some way from the house they met a little girl who belonged to Nikolai's family, and they asked her to run in and inquire whether they could talk to the gentleman. She ran as if her life depended on it, ran with both arms and legs, until she came to the door; then she put one foot on the high doorstep, fastened her garter, and rushed into the house; came back at once, leaving two doors open behind her, called out before she even reached the doorstep again that the gentleman would come immediately, whereupon she sat down beside the door with her back against the wall and looked out from under one arm at the strangers.

The gentleman came, and proved to be a tall, powerfully built person of twenty-some years. The counselor's daughter was a bit taken aback when she recognized in him the person who had sung in the rain. But he looked so pleasant and preoccupied; it was apparent from the expression in his eyes, from his hair, and from his hands, which were disoriented, that he had been reading a book.

The counselor's daughter curtsied gaily to him and cried "Peekaboo!" and laughed.

"Peekaboo?" asked the counselor.

But it was indeed the girlish face! The young man blushed deeply and tried to say something when the counselor put a question about the boat. Oh yes, it was at their disposal. But who should row? Why, he should, said the young lady. She didn't care what her father said; it made no difference that it caused the gentleman inconvenience, for he was sometimes not afraid of causing other people inconvenience. Then they walked down to the boat and provided the counselor with an explanation on the way. They got into the boat and were already quite a way out before the girl got herself comfortably settled and found time to talk.

"Well," she said, "you must have been reading something very learned when I came and said peekaboo and got you to go sailing."

"Rowing, you mean. Learned! It was *The Story of Sir Peter of the Silver Key and the Beautiful Magelone.*"

"Who wrote that?"

"It's by nobody; that kind of book never is. *Vigoleis with the Golden Wheel* is not by anybody, either. Neither is *Bryde the Marksman.*"

"I've never heard those titles before."

"Please move a little to one side, otherwise we can't get on an even keel. No, that's not surprising, they're not at all choice books; they are the sort you buy from vendors at fairs."

"That's strange. Do you always read books like that?"

"Always? I don't read many books in the course of a year, and I really prefer the kind of books with Indians in them."

"But works of literature? The works of Oehlenschäger, Schiller, and the others?"

"Oh yes, I know them all right; we had a whole bookcase full of them at home, and Miss Holm—my mother's companion—used to read aloud from them after lunch and in the evening; but I can't say that I cared for them—I don't like verse."

"Don't like verse! You said *used to*—isn't your mother still living?"

"No, and my father isn't either."

This was said in a somewhat somber, cold tone, and the conversation broke off for a while and permitted the many small sounds made by the boat's motion through the water to be heard clearly. The girl broke the silence.

"Do you like paintings?"

"Altarpieces? Oh, I don't know."

"Yes, or other pictures—landscapes, for example."

"Do they paint them, too? Oh yes, that's right; why, I know that.'"

"You're making fun of me, aren't you?"

"I! Well, one of us is being made fun of!"

"Aren't you a student?"

"Student! How would I have gotten to be a student? No, I'm nothing."

"Well, you have to be something. You must do something?"

"Why so?"

"Well, because—because everyone does."

"Do you do anything?"

"Oh yes, but you're not a lady."

"No, thank goodness!"

"Thanks!"

He stopped rowing, pulled the oars up a bit, looked her in the face, and said, "What do you mean by that? —No, you mustn't be angry with me; I'll tell you something—I'm an odd sort of person. You cannot understand that at all. You think I must be a genteel man because my clothes are so genteel. My father was a genteel man, and I've been told that he knew terribly much, and he probably did, too, since he was a district magistrate. I don't know anything, for Mother and I complied with each other's wishes in everything, and I didn't care about learning what you learn in school, and still don't. Oh, you should have seen my mother; she was such a tiny little lady. By the time I was thirteen years old, I could carry her out into the garden. She was so light that in her last years I often carried her in my arms all the way around the garden and the park. I see her now with her black dresses and wide lace. . . . "

He seized the oars and started rowing vigorously. The counselor became a bit uneasy when he saw the water rise so high at the stern and was of the opinion that they should see about getting back to land; and in they went.

"Tell me," asked the girl, when the vigorous rowing had slackened a bit, "do you often go to town?"

"I've never been there."

"Never been there! And you live only fourteen miles away."

"I don't live here all the time. I have been living all sorts of places since my mother died, but this winter I'm going to town in order to learn to calculate."

"Mathematics?"

"No, timber cargoes," he said, and laughed. "You don't understand that; so I'll explain. When I reach my majority, I want to buy a sloop and sail between here and Norway, and then I shall have to be able to calculate because of custom duties and clearances."

"Do you really want to do that?"

"It's so wonderful on the sea, there's such life in sailing. There's the dock." He drew alongside; the counselor and his daughter stepped ashore, after having made him promise that he would call on them at "Cape Trafalgar." Then, as he began to row across the lake, they went up to the county official's. Up by the poplars, they could still hear the strokes of the oars.

"Listen, Camilla," said the counselor, who had gone out to close the outer door. "Tell me," he said as he extinguished his hand lamp with the bit of his key, "was the rose the Karlsens had a Pompadour or a Maintenon?"

"Cendrillon," answered the daughter.

"That's right, that was the name—well—we must see about getting to bed. Goodnight, my dear, goodnight; sleep well."

When Camilla had come up to her room, she rolled up the blind, pressed her forehead against the cold pane, and hummed Elizabeth's song from the operetta *Elverhøj*. At sundown a light breeze had come up, and stray white clouds, illuminated by the moon, raced toward Camilla. She stood for a long time looking at them, followed them from afar with her eyes, and hummed louder and louder the nearer they came.

When they had disappeared overhead, she was silent for a few seconds, sought out new ones, then followed them. With a little sigh she rolled down the blind again. She went over to the dressing table, rested her elbows on it, placed her head on her folded hands and, without really seeing it, looked in the mirror at her image.

She thought of a tall young man who was walking with a little, sick, black-clad lady in his arms; she thought of a tall young man who was steering a little boat among rocks and skerries in a raging storm. She heard the entire conversation again. She blushed: Eugene Karlsen might have thought that you were courting him! By an association of ideas evoked by jealousy, she continued: Clara would never have been chased in the woods in the rain, would not have urged a stranger—literally urged him—to go boating with her in addition. "A lady to her fingertips," Karlsen had said about Clara; that was a reprimand to you, little Camilla, my country girl! Then she undressed with affected leisureliness, went to bed, took an elegant little book from the bookshelf by the bed, opened it to the first page, and read a little handwritten poem through with a tired and bitter expression, let the book fall to the floor, and burst into tears; then she gently picked the book up again, put it back in its place, and extinguished the light; she lay for a while and looked hopelessly at the moonlit blind, and finally went to sleep.

Not many days later, the "man in the rain" started off toward "Cape Trafalgar." A farmer who was driving a load of straw allowed him to ride along. For the first few miles he lay on his back in the straw and looked up at the cloudless sky, letting his thoughts come and go as they would; there was not much variety in them; most centered around how a person could be so wonderfully beautiful, and marveled at the fact that it could be a diverting occupation for several days to recall the features, expressions, and changes in the color of a face, the small movements of a head and a pair of hands, and the different modulations of a voice. But then the farmer pointed with his whip to a slate roof about a mile away and said that that was the counselor's. Mogens sat up in the straw and stared apprehensively at the roof, had a strange feeling of uneasiness, tried to imagine that nobody was home, but was tenaciously drawn to the notion that there was company there, and could not free himself of the notion, although he counted the number of cows grazing at Pleasaunce Manor and the number of piles of gravel he could see along the road. Eventually the farmer stopped where a small road ran down to the country house, and Mogens slid down from the load of straw. While the wagon ground its way down the gravel road, he began to brush off bits of straw. He approached the garden gate cautiously, saw a red shawl which disappeared behind the balcony windows, a small abandoned white sewing basket on the edge of the balcony, and the back of an empty rocking chair, still in motion. He stepped into the garden with his eyes still fixed on the balcony, heard the counselor say hello, turned his head toward the sound, and saw him standing there nodding, with his arms full of empty flowerpots. They exchanged a few words, and the counselor began to explain how one could say that, to a certain extent, the old caste difference between kinds of trees had been abolished by grafting, but that he was, incidentally, very much against the procedure. At this, Camilla came slowly toward them with a brilliant blue shawl about her. She had her arms wrapped in the shawl, and her greeting was a slight motion of the head and a faint "Welcome." The counselor went off with his flowerpots; Camilla stood and looked over her shoulder up at the balcony; Mogens looked at her. How had he been since they last met? Well, he couldn't complain. Rowed much? Oh yes, as was his custom; perhaps not quite so much. She turned her head toward him, looked coldly at him, cocked her head a little to one side, and asked with half-closed eyes and a faint smile whether it was the fair Magelone who had occupied his time. He didn't quite know what she meant. Then they stood for a time and said nothing. Camilla took a few steps to a corner of the garden where there was a bench and a garden chair; she sat down on the bench and, looking at the chair, invited him to sit down—he must be tired after the long, long walk. He sat down in the chair.

Did he think that something would come of the projected engagement in the royal house? That was perhaps a matter of indifference to him? Naturally, he didn't like the royal family? Of course, he hated the aristocracy? There were only a few young gentlemen who did not believe that democracy was God knows what. He was presumably among those who did not ascribe the connections of the royal house any political importance at all? Perhaps he erred, however. There had been cases, however. . . . She stopped suddenly, surprised that Mogens, who had at first been a little frightened at all this, now looked quite pleased. Was he sitting there laughing at her? She grew quite red.

"Are you very much interested in politics?" she asked uneasily.

"Not in the least."

"But why do you let me sit here and talk politics endlessly?"

"Oh, you say it all so beautifully, it doesn't make any difference what you're talking about."

"That's really no compliment."

"Why, indeed it is," he assured her eagerly, since it seemed to him that she looked offended.

Camilla burst out laughing, jumped up and ran to her father, took him by the arm, and walked with him over to the startled Mogens.

When the dinner was over and they had drunk coffee up on the balcony, the counselor suggested a stroll. The three of them walked down the little road, across the highway, down a narrow path with rye stubble on both sides, and over the stile into the enclosure. There stood the oak and everything else; there was even convolvulus still in the hawthorn hedge. Camilla asked Mogens to pick some of them for her. He tore them all off and came back with a whole handful.

"Thanks, I don't need so many," she said, taking a few of them, and letting the rest fall to the ground.

"In that case, I wish I had left them alone," said Mogens seriously.

Camilla bent down and began to pick them up again. She had expected that he would help her and looked up at him in surprise, but he stood quite motionless and looked down at her. Well, now that she had begun it, she had to continue, and gathered they were; but then she didn't talk to Mogens for a long, long time either, and didn't even look in his direction. But they must have become reconciled, for when, on their way home, they came to the oak again, Camilla went under it and looked up to its crown, tripped from one side to the other, flung out her arms, and sang, and Mogens had to go into the hazel bushes and see what a figure he had cut. All at once, Camilla ran toward him, but Mogens stepped out of character, forgot both to shout and to run, and Camilla declared, laughing, that she was very dissatisfied with herself and that she would not have believed herself daring enough to remain standing when such a dreadful person—and here she pointed to herself—came dashing toward her. But Mogens declared that he was very well satisfied with himself.

When he had to go home at sundown, the counselor and Camilla accompanied him a little way. And as they were returning, she told her father that they really ought to invite that solitary young man frequently during the month remaining, while it was still possible to stay in the country, for he didn't know anyone at all out here, and the counselor said yes, and smiled at being thought so naive, but Camilla looked gently serious in order to convince him that she was the personification of compassion itself.

The autumn weather was so mild that the counselor's household stayed on at Cape Trafalgar a whole month, and their compassion toward Mogens resulted in his coming there twice the first week and almost every day the third week.

It was one of the last days of good weather; it had rained early in the morning and had been overcast until late in the forenoon, but now the sun had come out and shone so strong and warm that the wet garden paths, the turf, and the branches of the trees were enveloped in a fine, light mist. The counselor was picking asters; Mogens and Camilla were over in one corner of the garden picking late winter apples. He was standing on a table with a basket on his arm; she was standing on a chair holding the corners of a large white apron.

"So what happened then?" she called impatiently to Mogens, who had broken off the story he was telling in order to get an apple hanging high up.

"Well," he continued, "then the farmer began to run around himself three times and to sing 'To Babylon, to Babylon, with an iron ring through my head,' then he and his heifer flew off with his great-grandmother and his black rooster; they flew over oceans as wide as Arup Ford, over mountains as high as Jannerup church, across Himmerland, through Holstein, right to the end of the world. There sat the troll, eating his breakfast; he finished just as they arrived.

" 'You should be a little more God-fearing, my good man,' said the farmer, 'otherwise it might happen that you will miss out on the Kingdom of Heaven.'

"Yes, he would like to be God-fearing.

" 'Then you must say a prayer of thanks,' said the farmer. . . . No, I don't want to tell any more," said Mogens impatiently.

"Then don't," Camilla said and looked at him in astonishment.

"I might just as well say it right now," continued Mogens. "I want to ask you something, but you mustn't laugh at me."

Camilla jumped down from the chair.

"Tell me—no, I want to say something myself—here is the table and there is the fence; if you won't be my fiancée, I'll run off with the basket, over the fence, and disappear. One!"

Camilla glanced up at him and saw the smile disappear from his face.

"Two!"

He was quite pale with emotion.

"Yes," she whispered, and released the corners of her apron so the applies skittered in all directions, and then she ran.

But she wasn't running away from Mogens.

"Three!" she said when he caught up with her, but he kissed her nevertheless.

They disturbed the counselor among his asters, but the magistrate's son was too nearly a matchless blend of nature and civilization for the counselor to raise any objections.

It was toward the end of winter; the heavy layer of snow, which was the result of a whole week's continual drifting, was in the process of rapidly melting away. The air was full of sunshine and glare from the white snow, which dripped down past the windows in large sparkling drops. Inside, in the parlor all the shapes and shades were awakened, all lines and contours came alive: that which was flat expanded, that which was bent grew arched, that which was slanting glided, and that which was broken became fragmented. All the green tones from the softest dark green to the sharpest yellow green, mixed luxuriantly on the flower stand.

The reddish brown tones flowed like flames over the surface of the mahogany table, and gold sparkled and glittered from the knickknacks, from the picture frames and the molding; but on the rug all colors were refracted in one merry, luminous confusion.

Camilla was sitting by the window and sewing, and she and the Graces on the console were quite enveloped in a reddish light from the red draperies. Mogens, who was pacing slowly up and down the room, passed continually in and out of slanting shafts of softly rainbow-hued dust particles.

He was in a talkative mood.

"Well," he said, "they're an odd sort of people you're associating with. There's nothing in the world they can't settle with a twist of the wrist—*this* is base and *that* is noble; *this* is the stupidest thing that's been done since the creation of the world, and *that's* the cleverest; *this* is so ugly, so ugly, and *that* is so beautiful that it's indescribable; and all this they're in agreement about —it's as if they had a certain table or something else by which they figured it out, for they all get the same answer, no matter what it is. How they resemble each other, those people! They all know the same thing, and they talk about the same thing; they all have the same vocabulary and the same opinions."

"You don't mean to say," Camilla objected, "that Karlsen and Rönholt are of the same opinion?"

"Yes, they're the nicest of the lot; they belong to different parties! Their basic views are as different as night and day! No, they're not; they are so much in agreement that it's funny; maybe there is some small point that they really disagree about, perhaps it's only a misunderstanding, but it is, heaven help me, pure comedy to listen to them; it's just as if they had agreed to do everything possible not to be in agreement. They begin by shouting and get excited right away; then one says something in his excitement that he doesn't mean; then the other says the exact opposite, which he doesn't mean either; and then the first one attacks what the second one didn't mean, and the second one that which the first one didn't mean; and then the game is started."

"But what have they done to you?"

"They annoy me, these fellows. When you look them in the face, it's as if you had a guarantee that in the future nothing remarkable will happen in the world."

Camilla put away her sewing, walked over to him, took hold of his coat collar, and looked roguishly and quizzically up at him.

"I can't stand that Karlsen," he said crossly, and tossed his head.

"Oh? So?"

"So you are so very, very sweet," he muttered comically and affectionately.

"So?"

"So," he burst out, "so he looks at you and listens to you and talks with you in a way I don't like; he's got to stop, he's got to, because you're *mine* and not *his*, aren't you? You're *not* his, not his at all. You *are* mine; you have made a pact with me, like the doctor with the devil; you're mine, body and soul, every inch, captive for all eternity." She nodded a little apprehensively and looked steadily up at him; tears came to her eyes, and she nestled up against him. He threw his arms around her, bent down, and kissed her on the forehead.

That evening Mogens accompanied the counselor to the station; orders had just come unexpectedly concerning a business trip the counselor was to undertake. Camilla was to go out to her aunt's the next morning and stay there until he returned.

When Mogens had sent his future father-in-law off, he walked homeward and thought about the fact that he would not see Camilla for several days. He turned into the street where she lived. It was long and narrow and there was little traffic. A coach rumbled away at the far end of the street; in the same direction there was the sound of footsteps fading away. Then the only sound he heard was a dog barking in the building behind him. He looked up at the house where Camilla lived; as usual it was dark on the ground floor, and the whitewashed panes received only a little uneasy life from the flickering glow of the streetlight on the neighboring house. Two flights up, the windows were open, and from one of them a dozen or so planks protruded over the sill. It was dark in Camilla's room. The floor above it was dark; only in the one attic window was there a golden glow from the moon. Above the house the clouds were in wild flight. In the buildings on both sides the windows were lighted.

The dark house made Mogens melancholy; it stood there so deserted and dreary. The open windows rattled on their fastenings; the water ran with a monotonous drumming into the gutters. Now and then a little water fell with a soft, hollow sound someplace where he could not see it, and the wind whistled mournfully down the street. That dark, dark house! Tears came to Mogens' eyes; it was as if there were a great weight on his chest, and he had a strange, vague feeling that he had something to reproach himself for concerning Camilla. Then he suddenly thought of his mother and felt a yearning to put his head in her lap and cry his fill.

He stood with his hand pressed to his chest a long time, until a carriage came at a quick pace down the street; he watched it and then went home. He had to tug repeatedly at the front door before it opened. Then he ran up the stairs humming, and once inside his room he threw himself on the sofa with one of Smollett's novels in his hand and read and laughed until past midnight.

At last it grew too cold in the room; he jumped up and stamped back and forth to drive away the chill. He stopped by the window; the sky was so light in the one direction that the snow-covered roofs merged into it; in the other direction some elongated clouds were drifting, and under them the sky had a strange reddish glow, an uncertain undulating glow, a red billowing fog; he threw open the window; fire had broken out over toward the counselor's house. Down the stairs, up the street as fast as he could, down a cross street, through a side street, and then straight ahead; as yet he could see nothing, but when he turned the corner he saw the fiery glow. A score of people clattered one by one down the street. In passing they asked each other where the fire was. The answer was "The refinery." Mogens continued running as fast as before, but with a much lighter heart. A few streets more; there were more and more people, and they were talking about the soap factory. It was across the street from the counselor's house. Mogens ran like mad. There was only one diagonal cross street to go, but it was completely filled with people—calm, well-dressed men, ragged old women who stood talking in drawn-out whining tones, shouting apprentices, gaily dressed girls whispering to each other, hangers-on standing motionless and cracking jokes, surprised drunkards and quarreling drunkards, helpless policemen, and hack drivers who could move their cabs neither forward nor backward. Mogens twisted his way through the mob. Now he was at the corner; the sparks slowly drifted down upon him. Up the street there were showers of sparks; to both sides the windowpanes glowed; the factory was on fire, the counselor's house was on fire, and the neighboring house was also on fire. Everything was smoke, fire, and confusion, shouting, cursing, roof tiles crashing down, ax-blows, splintering wood, rattling panes, jets of water that hissed, sputtered, and splashed, and through it all the regular, dull sobbing of the pump. Furniture, bedclothes, firemen's black helmets, ladders, shiny buttons, illuminated faces, wheels, cables, canvas, strange contrivances. Mogens rushed through it, over it, and under it all toward the house.

The facade was brightly illuminated by the flames from the burning factory; smoke trickled from between the roof tiles and poured out of the second story's open windows; the fire roared and crackled inside; there came a slow thundering sound which became a rumbling and cracking and ended with a dull boom; smoke, sparks, and flames were forced violently out of all the apertures of the house; and then the flames began to play and snap with redoubled strength and redoubled brightness. The central portion of the second-story ceiling fell. With both hands, Mogens seized a large fire ladder that was leaning against a part of the factory which was not yet in flames. For a moment it stood vertical, then it fell out of his grasp onto the counselor's house and smashed in a window frame on the third floor. Mogens sprang up the ladder and in through the opening. For a moment he had to close his eyes because of the acrid wood smoke. The heavy, choking fumes that rose from the charred timbers hit by streams of water took his breath away. He was in the dining room. The wall to the living room had almost entirely fallen away. The living room was one large glowing chasm, with flames from below reaching almost to the ceiling at times; the few boards that remained hanging after the floor had collapsed burned with clear yellowish white flames; shadows and the glare of flames undulated over the walls; the wallpaper curled up here and there, caught fire, and flew in burning flakes down into the chasm; and darting yellow flames licked upward to the loose molding and frames around the pictures. Mogens crawled over the fragments and pieces of the fallen wall to the edge of the chasm; from below, hot and cold currents of air alternately struck his face; on the other side, so much of the wall had fallen that he could look into Camilla's room, while the part of the wall which enclosed the counselor's office was still standing. It grew hotter and hotter; the skin on his face grew taut, and he noticed that his hair was curling. Something heavy brushed his shoulder, coming to rest across his back and pressing him to the floor; it was the crossbeam, which had slowly slid down out of place. He could not move, his breathing became heavier and heavier, his temples throbbed violently. To his left, a jet of water splashed against the wall of the dining room, and he was seized by the sole desire that the cold, cold drops which were spattering in all directions would strike him. Then he heard a groan on the other side of the chasm, and he saw something white moving on the floor in Camilla's room. It was she. She was on her knees, rocking back and forth, with her hands to her head. She rose slowly and came to the edge of the chasm. She stood rigidly upright, her arms hanging limply and her head seeming to oscillate on her neck. Very, very slowly the upper part of her body inclined forward until her beautiful long hair swept the floor; a sudden brilliant flash and it was gone; in the next moment she plunged down into the flames.

Mogens uttered a wailing sound, brief, deep, and strong, like the howl of a wild animal, and at the same time made a violent movement as if to get away from the chasm; he couldn't, because of the beam; his hands groped over the fragments of the wall and seemed to freeze in a powerful grasp about them, and then he struck his forehead rhythmically against the broken masonry and groaned, "My *God*, my *God*, my *God*!"

And so he lay there. After some time had passed, he noticed that something was taking hold of him; it was a fireman, who had cast the beam aside and wanted to carry him out of the house. Mogens noticed with a feeling of alarm that he was being lifted up and carried off. The fireman carried him to the opening; here Mogens had the clear impression that he was being harmed and that the fireman who was carrying him wanted to kill him. He tore himself loose from his arms, grasped a lath which lay on the floor, struck the fireman on the head with it and sent him reeling, came out of the opening, and ran down the ladder, holding the lath over his head. Through the turmoil, the smoke, the mob, through empty streets, across deserted squares to the field. Deep snow everywhere; not far off a black spot, a pile of gravel which protruded above the surface of the snow; he chopped at it with the lath, chopped at it again and again, continued to chop at it, wanted to chop it to pieces so it would disappear; he also wanted to run far away, then ran around and chopped at it like a madman; it wouldn't, it wouldn't go away; he slung the lath far from him and threw himself on the black pile to destroy it; he got his hands full of small stones; it was gravel, it was a black pile of gravel; why was he lying out in the field, clawing at a black pile of gravel?—He smelled the smoke, the flames flickered around him, he saw Camilla sink into them, he screamed and dashed off across the field. He could not rid himself of the sight of the flames; he covered his eyes—flames, flames! threw himself to the ground and pressed his face into the snow—flames! Sprang up, ran back, ran forward, ran in another direction—flames everywhere! Off across the snow, past houses, past trees, past a terrified face staring through a windowpane, around haystacks and through farmyards where dogs howled and tugged at their chains. He ran around the wing of a farmhouse and suddenly was standing in front of a window illuminated by a bright and flickering light. That light did him good; the flames gave way before it; he went over to the window and looked in; it was a scullery, a girl was standing at the hearth and stirring a kettle; the light she was holding in her hand shone reddish in the dense vapor; another girl was sitting and plucking poultry, and a third was singe-ing it over a blazing strawfire; the flames grew smaller; fresh straw was added, and they flared up again only to grow smaller once more, still smaller, and go out. Mogens angrily broke a windowpane with his elbow and walked slowly away; the girls inside screamed. Then he started running again, ran for a long time, whimpering softly. Scattered flashes of memory of happier days came, and it was doubly dark when they were gone; he could not bear thinking about what had happened; it could not have happened; he threw himself down on his knees and wrung his hands toward the heavens, begging that what had happened might be undone. For a long time he dragged himself along on his knees and kept his eyes fixed continuously on the heavens, as if he feared that they would slip away to evade his prayers if he did not continue looking at them. Then the images of happier days came to him; they hovered, more and more of them in misty, luminous sequences; there were also images that rose within him with a sudden radiance; and others flitted past, so indistinctly, so remotely, that they were gone before he knew what they were. He sat still in the snow, overcome by light and luminescence, by life and luck; and the vague fear which he had had in the beginning, that something would come and extinguish everything, had disappeared. It was so quiet about him, so calm within him; the images were gone, but the sense of happiness was there. So quiet! There was no sound—only ghost sounds. And there came laughter and song and fleeting words and fleeting footsteps and the dull sobbing of the pump strokes. Moaning, he ran off, ran long and far, came to the lake and followed its shore until the root of a tree tripped him; then he was so tired that he remained lying there.

With a soft, gurgling sound, water lapped over the small stones; the wind soughed lightly and intermittently through the bare branches; a few crows cawed out over the lake; the morning cast its glaring blue sheen over the woods and the lake, over the snow, and over the pale face.

At sunrise he was found by the ranger from the neighboring forest preserve and carried up to the house of Nicolai the gamekeeper. He lay there for weeks, hovering between life and death.

About the time Mogens was being taken to Nicolai's, a crowd was collecting around a carriage at the end of the street where the counselor lived. The coachman could not understand why the policeman wanted to keep him from carrying out his rightful task, and for that reason they were quarreling. It was the coach that was to take Camilla to her aunt.

"No! Since poor Camilla came to such a pitiful end, we haven't seen anything of him."

"Well, it's strange what can be hidden in a person. We didn't suspect anything, so dignified and shy, almost awkward. Isn't that right, ma'am, you *didn't* suspect the slightest thing?"

"About his sickness! Heavens, how can you ask such a question!—Oh, you mean . . . I didn't quite understand you . . . there was supposed to have been something in his blood, something hereditary?—Oh yes, I remember there was something about his father's being taken to Aarhus. Isn't that the way it was, Mr. Karlsen?"

"No!—Yes, but that was to be buried; his first wife is buried *there*. No, I was thinking, you know, of the terrible or . . . yes, the terrible life he has led these past two or two and a half years."

"Oh . . . um . . . um . . . no, I don't know anything about that."

"Well . . . yes . . . um . . . that's not the sort of thing one likes to talk about, one doesn't want to. . . . Well! You understand; out of consideration for others. . . . The counselor's family . . ."

"Yes, there *is* of course some justification for what you say . . . but on the other hand . . . tell me frankly, isn't there at times a false, a . . . pietistic attempt to veil, to conceal one's fellow men's weaknesses, and, of course I don't understand that sort of thing, but don't you think that the truth or public morals, I don't mean morality, but . . . morals, the state of affairs, whatever you want to call it, suffers as a result?"

"Absolutely! And I'm very pleased to be in agreement with you, and in this case. . . . The thing is simply this, that he has abandoned himself to all sorts of excesses, has lived in the most depraved way with the lowest sort of rabble, people without honor, without conscience, without standing, religion, or anything else, idlers, show people, tavern patrons and—if the truth must be told—loose women."

"And that after having been engaged to Camilla! My God! And after having been ill with brain fever for three months!"

"Yes—and what doesn't that tell you about his inclinations. And I wonder what his past was like. What do you think?"

"Yes, and the Lord knows how he really behaved during the very time of his engagement? There *was* something suspicious about him. Now that's *my* opinion."

"Excuse me, ma'am, and excuse me, Mr. Karlsen. You have interpreted the entire matter in the abstract, much in the abstract; I have by chance very concrete reports from a friend over in Jutland and can give an account of the matter in all its details."

"Mr. Rönholt! You wouldn't? . . ."

"Give details! Indeed I would, Mr. Karlsen, with the lady's permission. Thanks. He certainly hasn't lived as one should after having had brain fever. He has drifted from market town to market town with a couple of drinking companions, and is said not to have been without some connection with troupes of show people, and especially with their female members. Perhaps it would be best if I ran upstairs and fetched my friend's letter. If I may be excused? I'll be back in a moment."

"Don't you think, Mr. Karlsen, that Rönholt is unusually accommodating today?"

"Yes!—Undeniably. But you must also remember, ma'am, that he has vented his spleen in an article in the morning newspaper. Imagine, to dare to maintain . . . it's pure subversion, disregard for the law, for . . . hm . . . "

"You found the letter?"

"Yes, I did. May I begin? Let me see.—Oh yes! 'Our mutual friend whom we met last year in Mönsted and whom you said you knew from Copenhagen has for the last several months haunted the region hereabouts. He looks exactly the same as before; he is the same pale, sad knight of the sorrowful countenance. He is the oddest mixture of forced gaiety and quiet hopelessness, is affectedly inconsiderate and brutal toward himself and others, is quiet and taciturn and seems, although he does nothing but drink and daydream, not to enjoy himself at all; it is as I already said before, that he has the fixed idea of regarding himself as personally insulted by destiny. His special associates here were a horse trader called "the tavern deacon" because he was always singing and always boozing, and a swaggering, lanky cross between a sailor and a peddler known and feared under the name of "Wild Per," in addition to the fair Abelone; more recently she had to yield to a dark woman who belonged to a troupe of show people who for some time have regaled us with exhibitions of feats of strength and tightrope walking. You have seen that sort of women with sharp, yellowed, prematurely aged faces, people who have been wasted by brutality, poverty, and miserable vices, and who are always decked out in shabby velvet and dirty rouge. There you have the pack. I don't understand our friend's passion. It's true that his fiancée came to a pitiful end, but that doesn't explain things. You must hear how he left us. There was a market held several miles from here. He, Per, the horse trader, and the woman sat in a refreshment tent and boozed until far into the night. At three o'clock or so they were finally ready to leave. They get into their wagon and things go all right. But then our mutual friend turns off the highway and drives off with them over fields and moors as fast as the horses can go. The wagon is pitched from one side to the other. Finally it is too much for the horse trader, and he cries that he wants to get off. When he gets off, our mutual friend whips up the horses again and heads straight for a hill covered with heather; then the woman becomes frightened and gets off, and now it goes uphill and downhill at full speed so that it is a miracle that the wagon did not come down before the horses. On the uphill grade, however, Per had crept from the wagon, and as thanks for the ride he threw his large clasp knife at the driver's head.' "

"The poor fellow! But it is ugly about the woman."

"Despicable, ma'm, clearly despicable. Do you really think, Mr. Rönholt, that this report puts the man in a better light?"

"No, but in a more accurate one; you know, in darkness one can easily assume things to be larger than they are."

"Is anything worse thinkable?"

"If not, then this is the worst, but you know you should never believe the worst about people."

"Yes, you are of the opinion that it all isn't so bad, that there is something smart about it, something eminently plebeian which appeals to your inclination to the democratic."

"Can't you see that he acts quite aristocratically toward his surroundings?"

"Aristocratically! No, that's certainly paradoxical! If he's not democratic, I really don't know what he is."

"Well, there are also other definitions."

White chokeberry, bluish syringa, red hawthorn, and golden laburnum bloomed fragrantly outside the house. The windows were open and the Venetian blinds lowered. Mogens leaned in over the sill, the Venetian blinds resting on his back. It was refreshing for the eyes after all that summer sunshine in woods, water, and air to look into the living room's subdued, soft, soothing light. A tall, plump woman was standing inside with her back to the window, putting flowers in a large vase. The blouse of her pink housedress was gathered under her bosom by a black, shiny leather belt. On the floor behind her lay a snow-white mobcap; her abundant, very blond hair hung in a bright red snood.

"You're rather pale after the celebration last night," was the first thing Mogens said.

"Good morning," she answered, and without turning around stretched out her hand, with the flowers she happened to be holding, toward him. Mogens took one of the flowers. Laura half turned her head toward him, opened her hand slightly, and let the flowers fall to the floor a few at a time. Then she again turned to arranging the flowers in the vase.

"Sick?" asked Mogens.

"Tired."

"I'm not eating lunch with you today."

"You're not!"

"We can't have dinner together either."

"You're going fishing?"

"No!—Goodbye!"

"When are you coming again?"

"I'm not coming again."

"What's that supposed to mean?'" she asked, as she smoothed her dress and sat down on the chair by the window.

"I'm tired of you.—That's all there is to it."

"Now you're being malicious. What's wrong? What have I done?"

"Nothing, but since we are neither married nor madly in love with each other, I can't see that there's anything remarkable about my leaving."

"Are you jealous?" she asked very softly.

"Of somebody like you! God forbid!"

"But what does all this mean?"

"It means that I'm tired of your beauty, that I know your voice and your movements by heart, and that neither your moods nor your foolishness nor your slyness amuse me any longer. So can you tell me why I should stay?"

Laura wept. "Mogens, Mogens, how could you! What shall I, shall I, shall I, shall I do! Stay just today, just today—Mogens, you *mustn't* leave me!"

"Oh, that's nonsense, Laura; you don't believe that yourself. It's not because you think so much of me that you are upset; it's only a little uncertainty at the change, you are afraid of a little disturbance in your daily habits. I know that by past experience; you're not the first woman I've got tired of."

"Oh, stay with me today, I won't pester you to stay even another hour!"

"You're such curs, you women! You have no sense of pride; even if you're kicked away, you come crawling back again."

"We do, we do, but stay today.—Won't you—stay!"

"Stay, stay! No!"

"Oh, you've never loved me, Mogens."

"No!"

"Oh, yes, you have, you loved me that day the wind was so strong, that—that beautiful day down at the beach when we sat in the shelter of the boat—"

"Crazy girl!"

"If I were only a decent girl with high-class parents, and not the sort I am, you surely would stay with me, you wouldn't be so cruel—and I who love you so much!"

"You shouldn't!"

"No! I'm like the dirt you walk on, you don't care any more than that for me. Not a kind word, only cruel words; contempt, that's good enough for me."

"The others are neither better nor worse than you. Goodbye, Laura!"

He stretched out his hand toward her, but she kept her hands behind her back and whimpered, "No, no, not goodbye! Not goodbye!"

Mogens lifted the Venetian blind, took a couple of steps backward, and let it fall in front of the window. Laura quickly bent down and leaned out beneath it over the window sill and begged, "Come to me! Come and give me your hand."

"No!"

When he had gone a short distance, she cried out plaintively, "Goodbye, Mogens!"

He turned toward the house and waved. Then he went on. "And a girl like that still believes in love.—No, she *doesn't*."

The evening breeze blew from the sea over the land, and the beach grass swayed with its pale spikes and lifted its pointed blades slightly; the rushes tossed, the pond was darkened by thousands of tiny furrows, and the lily pads tugged restlessly at their stems. Then the dark tops of the heather began to flail, and on the sandy fields the sorrel swayed about disjointedly. In over the land! The sheaves of oats bent, the young clover trembled on the stubblefields, and the wheat rose and fell in heavy billows; the roofs bent, the mill creaked, the sails turned, the smoke was driven back down into the chimneys, and the window panes steamed over.

The wind soughed in the openings of the church towers, in the poplars of the manor, and whistled in the windswept scrub of Bredbjerg Grönhöj. Mogens lay up there and looked out over the dark earth. The moon was acquiring radiance; the mists drifted down there in the meadows. It was so melancholy, all of life, a void behind and darkness ahead. But such *was* life. Those who were happy were also blind. His eyes had been opened by misfortune; everything was unjust and deceitful; the entire world was one huge lie; loyalty, friendship, charity—lies, every bit of it was a lie—but what was called love, that was the hollowest of the hollow; lust is what it was, flaming lust, smoldering lust, reeking lust, but *lust* and never anything else. Why did he know all this? Why had he not been permitted to keep his faith in all these flame-gilded lies? Why should he be able to see and the others be blind? He had the right to blindness; he had believed in everything that could be believed in.

The lights were lit down in the town.

Down there was home upon home. My home! My home! And my childish faith in everything beautiful in the world! And what if they were right, the others? What if the world were full of beating hearts and heaven full of a loving God! Why don't I know *that*? Why do I know something different? I *do* know something different, so cutting, bitter, true. . . .

He got up; field and meadow were bathed in moonlight before him. He walked down toward the town by the path along the manor garden and looked over the stone wall. In the middle of a grassy plot in the garden stood a white poplar; the moonlight fell sharply on the trembling leaves that showed first their dark side and then their light. He put his elbows on the wall and stared at the tree; it looked as if the leaves were cascading over the branches. He thought he could hear the sound produced by the foliage. Nearby he heard a lovely feminine voice.

You blossom with dew,
You blossom with dew,
Whisper me dreams that are thine.
Is there in them the same air,
The same strange elfinland's air
As in mine?
Whispering, sighing, lamenting there;
Expiring fragrance, quiescent glare,
Awakening gong and budding song:
With longing,
With longing I live!

Then there was silence again. Mogens breathed deeply and listened intently: no song. Up at the manor house a door closed. Now he clearly heard the sound of the white poplar's leaves. He put his head on his arms and wept.

The next day was one of those of which late summer has so many. A day with a brisk, cool wind, perpetually growing dark and growing light as many large clouds drifted past the sun. Mogens had walked up to the cemetery; the manor garden bordered on it. It looked rather bare up there; the grass had recently been mowed; behind an old square iron grating stood a low spreading elder with fluttering leaves; about some of the graves were wooden frames; most of them were, however, only low, square mounds; some of them had metal plaques with inscriptions; others had wooden crosses from which the paint had peeled; others had wax wreaths; most of them had nothing at all. Mogens sought a spot which was out of the wind, but it seemed to be blowing on all sides of the church. He threw himself down near the embankment and took a book out of his pocket, but his attempt at reading came to nothing; every time a cloud passed before the sun the air seemed to grow too cold and he thought of getting up again, but then the sun came out once more and encouraged him to remain lying there. A girl approached slowly, with a greyhound and a pointer running and playing ahead of her. She stopped and seemed to want to sit down, but when she caught sight of Mogens, she continued her walk diagonally through the cemetery and out the gate. Mogens got up and watched her; she was walking down on the highway, and the dogs were still playing. Then Mogens began reading the inscription over one of the graves; it made him smile. Suddenly a shadow passed over the grave and stopped. Mogens looked to that side. There stood a sunburned young man, one hand in his game bag, the other hand holding a gun.

"That's not so bad, that one," he said, and nodded toward the inscription.

"No," said Mogens, straightening up.

"Tell me," continued the hunter, and he looked to one side as if searching for something, "you've been here a couple of days, and I've been wondering about you, but I haven't been close enough to talk to you until now. You've been wandering around alone, why haven't you dropped in on us? And how in the world do you pass the time? You're not on business in the area?"

"No, I'm staying here for my own pleasure."

"Well, there's certainly plenty of that here," the stranger exclaimed and laughed. "Don't you go hunting? Wouldn't you like to go with me? I have to go down to the inn and get some shot anyway, and while you're getting ready, I can go over and nag the blacksmith. Well, will you come along?"

"Gladly!"

"But that's right—Thora! Haven't you seen a girl?" He sprang up on the embankment. "Yes, there she goes. She's my cousin. I can't introduce you, but come on, let's follow her. We made a bet; now you can be the judge. She was to be in the cemetery with the dogs, and I was to walk past with my gun and game bag and could neither call nor whistle, and if the dogs came to me anyway, she would lose. Now we'll see."

They soon overtook the lady; the hunter looked straight ahead, but he could not help smiling. Mogens nodded as they went past. The dogs looked surprised after the hunter and growled slightly, then they looked up at the lady and barked; she wanted to pet them, but they walked away from her indifferently and barked at the hunter; they walked farther and farther away, glanced back at her, and then set off all at once after the hunter and when they reached him became completely unmanageable, jumping on him and darting off in all directions and back again.

"You've lost!" he called to her. She nodded, smiling, turned about, and left.

The hunt lasted until late in the afternoon; Mogens and William got along well together, and Mogens had to promise to come to the manor house in the evening. That he did, and went there nearly every day after that. But despite all offers of hospitality, he continued to live at the inn.

This was an unsettled time for Mogens. At first Thora's presence awakened all the sad and oppressive memories; often he suddenly had to talk with someone else or leave so that his emotions would not overcome him completely. She didn't resemble Camilla at all; nevertheless, he heard and saw only Camilla. Thora was small, delicate, and slight, smiled easily, cried easily, and grew enthusiastic easily. If she talked to someone seriously for any length of time, it was not a sign of intimacy, but rather of being lost in her own thoughts. If someone told or explained something to her, her face, her entire being, expressed the most sincere trust and sometimes even expectation. William and his little sister treated her not exactly as a comrade, yet certainly not as a stranger. Her uncle and aunt, the hired men and girls, all the country people of the area paid court to her, but very carefully, and almost fearfully. Their attitude toward her was almost like that of someone who while strolling through the woods sees at close range an exquisite little songbird with bright, intelligent eyes and small, graceful movements; one is delighted with the little living creature, wants so much for it to come closer and closer, but doesn't dare move or even breathe lest it should be frightened and fly away.

As Mogens saw Thora more and more often, the memories came less and less frequently, and now he began to see her as she was. It was a time of peace and happiness when he was with her, of silent longing and silent sadness when he did not see her. Later he talked with her about Camilla and his past, and it was almost with astonishment that he looked back upon himself; sometimes it was almost incomprehensible to him that it was he who had thought, felt, and done all the strange things he told about.

One evening he and Thora were looking at the sunset from a little knoll in the garden. William and his little sister were playing tag around the rise. There were light, bright colors by the thousands, strong and radiant ones by the hundreds. Mogens turned away from them and looked at the dark figure at his side: how insignificant she appeared compared with all this glowing splendor. He sighed and looked again at the many-colored clouds. It was not really an idea, but something remote and fleeting, there for a second and then gone; it was as if the eye had thought it.

"The trolls in their green hillock are happy now that the sun is all the way down," said Thora.

"Oh?"

"Why yes! Don't you know that trolls love darkness?"

Mogens smiled.

"Well, you don't believe in trolls, but you really should. It's so nice to believe in all that, in hillock people and elfin maids. I also believe in mermaids and wood nymphs; but elves! What does one do with elves and birds of ill omen? Old Maren gets angry when I say that, for there is no piety in believing in that, she says, that which I believe in, something that doesn't have to do with people; but portents and church goblins, they're in the Gospels, she says. But what do you say?"

"I? Well, I don't know.—What do you really mean?"

"You must not like nature."

"Why? Quite the contrary!"

"Well, I don't mean nature when it is ceremoniously served up, the way you see it from a bench with a scenic view, with hills and trails leading up them, but nature every day, always. Do you like nature that way?"

"Precisely! Every leaf, every twig, every beam of light, every shadow I can enjoy. There's no hill so barren, no peat pit so square, no highway so dull that I can't fall in love with it for a moment."

"But what pleasure can you have from a tree or a bush if you can't imagine that it contains a living creature that opens and closes the flowers and smoothes the leaves? When you see a lake, a deep and clear lake, isn't the reason you like it that you imagine that deep, deep down inside there are creatures that have their pleasures and sorrows, their own strange life with strange longings? And what is pretty about Bredbjerg Grönhöj when you don't imagine that it is teeming and humming with tiny, tiny creatures that sigh when the sun rises but begin to dance and play with their beautiful treasures when evening comes?"

"How strangely beautiful! And you see all that?"

"But you?"

"Well, I can't explain it, but it has something to do with the color, the movement, and the form it has, and also the life that it contains, the juices that rise in trees and flowers, the sun and the rain which make them grow, and the sand that drifts to form knolls, and cloudbursts that furrow and cleave the steep slopes.—Oh! It doesn't make sense when *I* try to explain it."

"Is that enough for you?"

"Oh, it's sometimes too much! Far too much! When there's form and color, as well as movement, so lovely and so graceful, and beyond all this there is a mysterious world that lives and exults and sighs and yearns, and which can express all this in word and song, then you feel so forsaken when you can't approach that world, and life grows so dull and oppressive."

"No, no! You mustn't think of your fiancée that way."

"Oh, I'm not thinking of my fiancée."

William and his sister came up to them and they went inside together.

One morning several days later, Mogens and Thora were walking in the garden. Mogens was going to see the greenhouse where the grapes were grown; he had not been *there* yet. It was a long, not very high greenhouse; the sun sparkled and played on the glass roof. They walked inside; the air was warm and moist and had a strangely heavy and aromatic odor, like fresh topsoil. The beautiful sinuous leaves and the heavy dewy bunches of grapes, made translucent and luminous by the sun, were spread out under the glass roof in a single blissful expanse of green. Thora stood happily looking up; Mogens was restless and stared now sadly at her, now up into the foliage.

"Listen," said Thora cheerfully, "now I think I'm beginning to understand what you said before on the knoll about form and color."

"Is that all you understood?" Mogens asked softly and seriously.

"No," she whispered, looked at him quickly, lowered her eyes, and blushed. "Not then."

"Then!" Mogens repeated gently and knelt before her. "But now, Thora?"

She bent down toward him, extended one hand to him and held the other to her eyes and wept. Mogens pressed her hand against his breast as he arose; she lifted her head and he kissed her forehead. She looked up at him with radiant, moist eyes, smiled, and whispered, "Thank God!"

Mogens stayed another week; the agreement was that the marriage would take place at midsummer. Then he left, and then winter came with dark days, long nights, and a snowstorm of letters.

Lights in all the windows of the manor, leaves and flowers over all the portals, smartly dressed friends and acquaintances densely crowded on the broad stone steps, all staring out into the twilight—Mogens had driven away with his bride.

The carriage rumbled and rumbled; the closed windows rattled; Thora sat and looked out through one of them at the side of the road, at the blacksmith's hill, where there were primroses in the spring, at Bertel Nielsen's large elderberry bush, at the mill and the miller's geese, at Dalum slope, where she and William had gone sledding not so many years ago, at Dalum meadows, at the long fantastic shadows of the horses which darted over the piles of gravel, over the pits in the bog, over the rye field. She sat and wept silently; now and then when she dried the moisture from the windowpane, she glanced over at Mogens. He sat leaning forward with his coat open; his hat lay swaying on the front seat; he held his hands before his face. What all *he* had on his mind! It had been a strange day for him, and the leave-taking had almost exhausted his courage. She had had to say goodbye to all her relatives and friends, to an endless number of places where memories and recollections lay one on another all the way up to heaven—and this in order to leave with him. And he was a dependable person to submit oneself to, he with his past of coarseness and dissipations! It wasn't so certain that this was behind him; to be sure, he had changed and had difficulty understanding what he himself had been, but you never escape completely from yourself; it *was* all still there, and here he had this innocent child to keep and care for, thank God! He had managed to get himself sunk in the mire; he would doubtless succeed in getting her down there too. No! No, she must not.—No, she must be allowed to live her carefree, gay, girlish life despite him. And the carriage rumbled and rumbled; darkness had descended, and now and then he caught a glimpse, through the steamy windows, of the lights in the farms and houses they drove past. Thora dozed. Toward morning they came to their new home, an estate Mogens had bought. The horses steamed in the cold morning air, the sparrows chirped in the big lindens in the courtyard, and the smoke wreathed slowly from the chimneys. Thora smiled and looked happily at everything after Mogens had helped her down; but it couldn't be helped, she *was* sleepy and too tired to conceal it. Mogens accompanied her to her room and then went out into the garden alone, sat down on a bench, and thought that he was watching the sunrise, but he was nodding too much to persevere in that belief.—At dinner time, he and Thora again met, happy and refreshed, and there was a tour of the estate and much astonishment; plans were laid and decisions reached and the most foolish suggestions were made which were unanimously declared to be practical, and how Thora strove to look intelligent and interested when the cows were presented to her, and how difficult it was not to become all too impractically happy over a woolly little puppy; and Mogens, how *he* talked about drainage and grain prices while he stood and speculated on how Thora would look with red poppies in her hair!

And then in the evening when they sat in their sun parlor, and the moonlight so precisely outlined the windows on the floor, what sort of comedy was this on his part when he seriously suggested to her that she should go to bed, really go to bed, for she *must* be tired, while he continued to hold her hand in his; and on her part when she declared that he was monstrous and wanted to get rid of her, that he regretted having married; and then there was naturally a reconciliation, and they laughed until the hour grew late. Finally Thora went to her room, but Mogens remained sitting in the sun parlor, grossly unhappy that she had gone; and then he created grim fantasies that she was dead and gone, and that he was sitting there quite alone in the world, weeping for her; and then he really wept. Then he was angry with himself, paced the floor, and tried to be reasonable. There *was* love, pure and noble, totally without coarse, worldly passion; yes, there was, and if there wasn't, it would come; yes, passion ruined everything, and it was so ugly, so inhuman! How he hated everything in human nature that wasn't chaste and pure, delicate and genteel! He had been cowed, oppressed, and plagued by this ugly and powerful force; it had possessed his eyes and ears and had poisoned all his thoughts. He went into his room. He wanted to read and picked up a book; he read without having any idea what he was reading.—Surely nothing could have happened to her! No, why that? He grew fearful nevertheless. It might be—. No, he could not stand it; he stole silently to her door; no, it was so quiet and so peaceful; when he listened intently, it seemed to him that he could hear her breathing.—How his heart was pounding; he thought he could hear that too. He returned to his room and his book. He closed his eyes; how clearly he saw her; he could hear her voice; she bent down to him and whispered—. How he loved her, loved her, loved her! It sang within him; it was just as if his thoughts came rhythmically; and how clearly he could envisage everything that he was thinking of! Silently, silently she lay there and slept, with her arm behind her head, her hair loose, her hair loose. Her eyes were closed, she breathed so softly—the air trembled, there was a shimmer of red like the reflection from roses.—Like a clumsy faun who is imitating a nymph's dance, the blanket reproduced in coarse folds her graceful figure.—No, no! He didn't want to think of her, not think of her that way, not for anything in the world, no, and here it all came again. It *could* not be kept away, but it had to be, away, away! And it came and went, came and went, until sleep came and night went.

As the sun was going down the next evening, they walked around the garden together. Arm in arm, they walked very slowly and very quietly up one path and down another, out of the fragrance of mignonettes through the fragrance of roses into the fragrance of jasmine. A few moths fluttered past, a wild bird called out in the grainfield; otherwise the loudest sound came from Thora's silk dress.

"How silent we can be!" exclaimed Thora.

"And how we can walk!" continued Mogens. "We must have walked five miles."

They continued walking for a time and were silent.

"What are you thinking about?" she asked.

"I'm thinking of myself."

"That's just what I'm doing."

"You're also thinking of yourself?"

"No—of yourself—you, Mogens."

He drew her closer to him. They approached the sun parlor. The door was open; it was brightly lit inside, and the table with its snowy cloth, the silver platter with dark red strawberries, the gleaming silver pitcher, and the candelabra made a festive impression.

"It's just like the fairy tale where Hansel and Gretel came to the gingerbread house out in the woods," said Thora.

"Would you like to go in?"

"You're forgetting that there is a witch inside who will roast and eat us unfortunate little children. No, it's much better that we resist the sugary windows and pancake roof and take each other by the hand and go out into the dark, dark woods."

They walked away from the sun parlor. She pressed against Mogens and cautioned, "It can also be the grand vizier's palace and you are the Arab from the desert who wants to carry me off, and the guard is after us; scimitars are flashing, and we run and run, but they've captured your horse, and then they capture us too and put us in a big sack and there we sit together and are drowned in the ocean.—Let me see, what more is there? . . ."

"Why can't it be the way it is?"

"That would be all right, but it's not enough. . . . If you only knew how I love you, but I'm so unhappy . . . I don't know what it is . . . there's such a distance between us . . . . No . . . ."

She threw her arms around his neck and kissed him impetuously and pressed her burning cheek against his. "I don't understand it, but sometimes I almost wish that you would strike me.—I know it's childish, and that I'm so happy, so happy, but all the same I'm *so* unhappy!"

She laid her head on his breast and wept, and while the tears were flowing she began to hum, at first quite softly, then louder and louder.

> With longing,
> With longing I live.

"My own little wife!" and he lifted her in his arms and carried her inside.

In the morning he stood by her bed. The light came, tranquil and subdued, through the lowered shades, and it lent elegance to the contours of the room and imparted fullness and serenity to all the colors. To Mogens it was as if the air rose and fell with her bosom, in a gentle swell. Her head rested obliquely on the pillow, her hair lay across her white forehead, one cheek was deeper red than the other. Now and then her gently arched eyelids quivered slightly, and the lines of her mouth wavered imperceptibly back and forth between unconscious seriousness and slumbering smiles. Mogens stood for a long time looking at her, happy and composed, the last of the shadows from his past gone. Then he stole softly out and sat down in the living room and waited quietly for her. He had sat there for a time when he felt her head on his shoulder and her cheek against his.

They went out together into the freshness of the morning. The sunlight frolicked over the earth, the dew sparkled, early wakening flowers were radiant, the lark trilled high in the heavens, the swallows darted through the air. He and she walked off across the green paddock toward the hill with the ripening rye; they followed the path which ran through it; she walked ahead very slowly and looked back over her shoulder at him, and they talked and laughed. The farther they came down the hill, the more they were hidden by the grain, and soon they could not be seen anymore.

Henrik Pontoppidan

Den kongelige Gæst (The Royal Guest, 1908) was the last in a long series of very short novels that Pontoppidan had begun in 1885. Many of these appeared prior to the publication of the two multi-volume works, *Det forjættede Land* (The Promised Land, 1891–95) and *Lykke-Per* (Lucky Per, 1898–1904). A revised version of "Den kongelige Gæst" was included in a collection of Pontoppidan's short stories and sketches issued in 1922. In 1919 an opera was made by Hakon Børresen. In 1922 the story was rewritten as a play by Carl Gandrup.

The present translation is of Pontoppidan's final version of the story.

The Royal Guest

I

When people who tumble about in the bustle of a big city think now and then—perhaps with a little sigh of longing—of life in the country, there hovers in their minds the picture of an existence blessed with leisure. They imagine an endless series of quiet days in which every minute passes with the imposing serenity of a grandfather's clock that measures eternity in the parlor of an old farmhouse.

And in reality, there is no place where time is more fleeting and where life seems shorter than in the country. Even if the individual days may be prosaic enough in their uniformity, the weeks are in a hurry—the years flee. One fine day life is over and everything disappears like a remnant of a summer or winter night's dream.

Whenever the young physician Arnold Hojer and his pretty little wife remembered that they had been in Sønderbøl for six whole years and had been married exactly the same length of time, they had to laugh with surprise. Six years! They felt that it was impossible that any more than six months could have elapsed since that unforgettable, starry night when they arrived on the stagecoach. They had nevertheless brought three children into the world in the interim, and their house, which at first was an indifferent piece of workmanship that still smelled of moist lime, had been the very center of the earth and the threshold to heaven.

They both belonged to Copenhagen, and in the midst of their great love and happiness both of them had in the beginning been quiet but despondent. The many new conditions and the curious customs, even the treeless Jutland landscape with its vastness of sky, made them as bewildered as a pair of stray kittens.

Emmy had sometimes felt tears come to her eyes when she but thought of Copenhagen. When Arnold was making a call, she sat in his room with an oppressive feeling of loneliness and did nothing but await his return.

How strange it was to think of those days now! Could she really have been so childish! There she had sat at the window, with her cheek resting solemnly on her hand, staring out over the dark, heathered hills with the giddy feeling that she had been left alone on a strange planet far out in the unending universe.

A more lonesome spot than Sønderbøl would be difficult to find. It was twenty miles to the nearest railway station. A stagecoach served as the connecting link with the outside world, but they never even saw it. The big yellow coach with its scarlet-clad coachman, which might have enlivened the landscape a bit, passed through the village at night both to and from its destination. It served only to enhance their dreams when it rolled past on the country roads in the dark nights, its gleaming light trailed across the windowshade in the bedroom.

The village itself was composed of seven or eight scraggly farmhouses and twice that number of wretched huts. It harbored no pastor and his family—only a schoolteacher, who had proved to be a cantankerous fellow at that.

During the first year, they had been visited several times by their families and friends, who were curious to see how they had adapted themselves out in their wilderness. In the second year the visits had been less frequent, although, for that matter, they did not miss them any more. Now, after six years, they were no longer conscious of their loneliness.

They simply had no time for that. Emmy was engrossed with her home and her children, and when Arnold was not away on calls, he was busy out in the garden, or he stood sweating over the wood box, since, for the sake of exercise, he sawed and split for firewood everything they could gather in this treeless landscape. Aside from this, they received several daily newspapers for diversion, and during the winter they subscribed to a private book club, which brought a peck of the season's best literature every fortnight.

It was written on their faces both in lines and in color that they were thriving and satisfied. Inside the wooden fence which surrounded their house and garden and gave them shelter from the west, there grew up a little earthly Eden, where a little Cain and a little Abel were bronzed by sun and wind, while a year-old daughter of Eve with blond locks rode pickaback on her mother, and where various sorts of useful and prolific animals quacked, cackled, and grunted out in the farmyard and in the farm buildings.

If only their neighbor, Sørensen, the schoolteacher, and his glassy-eyed wife had not existed, they would have felt themselves completely happy.

One day in February, after they had not heard from their relatives in Copenhagen for a long time, there came a letter from Emmy's three cousins, announcing an impending visit during the pre-Lenten period.

It was not exactly the best time of year for the display of their glory. There was snow in the garden, and indoors there was gradually less and less room, so that it was a tight squeeze to provide extra beds. But Emmy always found an expedient. Like a conjuror she grappled with sofas and beds and at the same time made elaborate preparations in the kitchen. The guests would have no other impression than that they were welcome, she said. Furthermore, she felt it was a sort of mission to show these city-dwellers how able and healthy one could become out on the Jutland heath.

There was the devil to pay the day that the guests were expected. The house stood festively ready for the reception, and the sheets had been draped on chairs around the ovens to dry them thoroughly when the telegram of regret came. Difficulties had arisen at the last moment. The visit would have to be postponed until a future date.

Arnold was making a call when the telegram came. Emmy received it and had to laugh, as annoyed as she actually was. Resolutely, she gave the maids orders to put everything back in its usual place at once and when Arnold came home at noon, the house had already been brought into its accustomed order. To avert an all too violent exclamation of irritation, Emmy met him at the door with a broad smile.

But that did not help. Arnold, who was a hothead, felt himself personally offended by every bit of bad luck. When he had read the telegram, his face became pale yellow where it was not covered by his beard; he shouted about impudent thoughtlessness.

Emmy really thought just as he did, but she could not take that sort of thing so seriously.

"We will talk no more about that, Arnold!" she said finally. "Come in now and eat! We have food enough in the house now, at least."

After supper, as was their custom, they sat in Arnold's room and talked together in the twilight while the nursemaid superintended the small boys in the dining room on the other side of the hall. Arnold's temper had cooled. With his long pipe he sat—well fed—in the rocking chair by the stove and made himself comfortable in his housecoat and felt slippers.

Emmy sat at the window and held her little girl in her lap. The pudgy child lay on its back and kicked complacently with its bare legs while its diapers were changed. Outside there was a heavy snowfall. It had been snowing lightly all day, but now it was falling in earnest. Already there lay a border of snow an inch high on the windowsill and on the crossbars of the window. Winter only increased their feeling of security and comfort and brought them a sensation of warmth and solidity.

Emmy had not had time to change her clothes. She was still in her morning dress and her hair was done up in a piece of black veil. The years had made her a bit negligent about her appearance, despite the fact that she had not lost her beauty since her marriage. Her small, plump figure with her dark brown eyes and heavy eyebrows—"the owl," her friends had called her of old—was amazingly unchanged; it had at the most attained a more motherly form and a somewhat softer contour.

"Do you know," she said, while playing with the child, "I'm not sure that we should be distressed that they are not coming. It would perhaps not have been so pleasant with that run of visitors. I realize now that I haven't felt myself really at home in my own house in the last few days."

Arnold lowered his eyes from the clouds of tobacco smoke and had to smile. As it so often happened, she had again said exactly what he had been thinking. If he had not just been out of his chair a moment before to find a match, she would have received a kiss for those words.

They sat for some time and chatted about this and that. They talked about what had happened in the village, discussed their own domestic problems, spoke about the children and about a new breed of chicken which they intended to introduce to the region—topics about which they had not been able to exchange opinions in the last few days because of the disturbed household conditions.

Suddenly Emmy exclaimed: "That's right! I had forgotten to tell you! This morning I saw old Thorvald Andersen go into the school building with a piece of paper in his hand. Do you think that that could be the petition?"

Arnold's pipe slid out of his mouth. For a moment he stared open-mouthed.

When he regained his speech, his brow was creased like a plowed field up to the roots of his hair.

"Listen, Emmy. If that schoolteacher Sørensen is serious about that petition and sends it in to the parish council, there's going to be war. I *will* not have his disgusting waste water out in our ditch. If *he* goes to the parish council, then *I* shall appeal to the board of health; and I shall submit, just as I did before, an enclosure which has teeth in it. You can be sure of that!"

"Yes, if you only would! Oh, I should like to see that ugly fellow get a slap in the face. By the way, did I tell you? Yesterday, when I was at the store, who should be standing there in the middle of the floor but Adolfine herself. Heavens! You should have seen her! One, two, three, and she turned her back. Of course I pretended nothing had happened and went up to her and said how are you and asked about the children—that was a great bit of playacting, you can be sure."

From the dining room was heard weeping and quarreling. The twilight had made the boys sleepy. Emmy got up in order to light the lamp and at the same time to put the baby to bed.

When she came back, Arnold had lighted the hanging lamp and pulled the curtain in front of the window. He was standing at the smoking stand, filling his pipe, but turned his glance toward the living room.

"Do you know what I am standing here thinking of, Emmy? We mentioned the other day that it was a little crowded in the living room. What would you say to our pushing the bookcase there a little farther toward the door and then setting the oval pedestal here in the corner with the bust on it. That would liven things up!"

"No, you're impossible, Arnold! Don't you think that we have rummaged about enough here in the house during the last few days? Let me have some peace."

"Now, now. You don't need to make a fuss. It was only a suggestion, you know."

"Yes indeed, but it has really become a sort of mania with you. I believe that you are suffering from a sort of moving sickness."

"And you have become a regular setting hen, Emmy. Soon you will not allow a chair in the house to be moved."

"No—why should it be?"

Arnold laughed.

"Do you remember when I proposed last year to move the garden house to the west for the sake of the view? You fought against it tooth and nail—you said that there was more wind there, which I denied. Now you must concede that I was right."

This time it was Emmy who had to laugh. She went to Arnold and put her hand on his shoulder.

"No, dear, sweet little Arnold—that I really can't concede. Why, we couldn't be there all summer because of the draft. You cannot have forgotten that."

"I have not forgotten that you continued to assert that was so. But that is something quite different."

She turned away from him.

"Oh, you don't mean that yourself. You just will not admit that you were wrong. I have said so many times."

"Listen, Emmy, if you keep on with that stupid assertion, I'll take the whole garden house down. I'm tired of hearing such complaints. Then you and the children can be happy."

He took a newspaper and seated himself at the table with his back toward her. She started to dust, humming as she did so, as was her custom when she had been offended and her spirits became like the sultry weather before a storm.

At this point, the tension in the atmosphere was relieved by the sound of a sleigh which stopped outside the house.

"Someone has probably sent for you," said Emmy. And she added in a conciliatory fashion, "In such weather!"

Arnold had raised his head. "That must be the pastor! Don't you hear? Those are horses with bells."

A few minutes passed. Then the maid slipped through the door from the hall, so fascinated that she forgot to set down the lamp. Breathless, she reported that there was a strange gentleman outside, who was enquiring whether anyone was home.

"Did he give his name?"

No—he had just asked after the doctor and his wife.

"Oh, of course it's the pastor's brother-in-law—the surveyor."

Oh no! It was a total stranger. And a terribly fine gentleman it was for sure. She thought that it was probably the new bishop, who had been there on inspection last summer.

"Oh—nonsense!" said Arnold, who nevertheless looked down at his clothes, perturbed.

Emmy was also troubled at the thought of her costume, which was not meant to be seen by strangers.

"You will have to stay here and receive him," she said, and disappeared hastily through the door to the living room.

Arnold put down his pipe and gathered his housecoat around him as well as possible in order to conceal the shortcomings of his dress. Through the half-open door, he saw on the wall of the vestibule the shadow of a large man, who, with the aid of the maid, pulled off a pair of large fur boots and then slipped off an overcoat.

In a moment the personage appeared in the door.

II

He was a man of medium height about fifty years of age, with a wreath of curly grayish brown hair around a high, bald pate. An exceptionally well-dressed man in a long, black cutaway coat with large silk lapels. A man, who, despite his unusual circumference, made absolutely no humorous or unpleasant impression. A man of carriage. Really a rather good-looking man, fit and ruddy-cheeked, with a pair of lively, light brown eyes and a youthful mouth full of large white teeth.

"Is it Dr. Hojer I have the honor of greeting?" he asked as Arnold approached him.

"Yes, won't you have a seat."

They sat down on either side of the table under the hanging lamp and now, when Arnold saw him in full light, the guest seemed even younger. Arnold took him to be—despite his girth—at the most forty-odd. He could just barely detect a resemblance to the new bishop. Otherwise, there was not the slightest characteristic about the man which suggested the clergy. If he had not worn a little cropped mustache and a correspondingly small, pointed beard on his lower lip, and if his dress and behavior had not been so completely those of a gentleman, Arnold would have mistaken him for an actor from some traveling company.

"You have come from Jerrild," he said, while he wondered why the stranger had not yet introduced himself.

With a start, the expression on the stranger's face darkened fleetingly. He seemed to want to hide an unpleasant surprise. The next moment he smiled again with all his white teeth.

"You really surprise me, doctor! I do not understand how you can know—. I must believe that you possess that magic mirror which fairy tales tell of."

"Oh no, the explanation is really very simple. Pastor Jørgensen is the only one hereabouts who drives a sleigh with big bells. The farmers all have small bells."

"Oh—I see! Yes, and I may just as well confess. But first you must permit me to present a request which probably will seem very peculiar to you. I would like to ask, doctor, that you excuse me from an introduction of my civil person and give me permission to appear before you as an out-and-out nameless traveler. Yes, I see that you are taken aback. You even think perhaps that it is a crazy man whom you have before you. But I assure you, I have quite intelligent reasons for my request."

"I do not doubt that," declared Arnold with an awkward smile. The artificial language of social intercourse had become unfamiliar to him. He was not sure whether the man's words should be taken literally or were perhaps an elegant way of speaking.

"You will no doubt understand, doctor, that when I attempt to excuse, or at least explain, my rash presence here—my impudent intrusion, which you probably in your own quiet thoughts feel . . ."

"By no means," murmured Arnold, becoming more and more uncertain.

"Oh well! Short and to the point: Pastor Petersen in Jerrild is my old boyhood friend. . . . "

"Petersen?" said Arnold. "There is no Pastor Petersen in Jerrild."

"Pardon me?—Oh, that's right!—You cannot know that. But he really is called Petersen."

"Is Pastor Jørgensen called Petersen?"

The stranger laughed aloud.

"Yes, that is, we—all his childhood friends—have always called him that. The reason for it is that he once—half in fun—complained about his commonplace name. We decided then that we should in the future call him Petersen. And we were so pleased with that joke that we have never been able to forget it. I have not seen my dear, boyhood friend for many years now, and it has long been my desire to surprise him some day in his idyllic parsonage. But I have not been lucky in my choice of a day. When I arrived there this afternoon, the family had just left and was not expected back until some time tonight."

"Oh, now I understand!" said Arnold.

"Yes, doctor, I must confess that I belong to those of a social nature. The prospect of having to spend a long winter evening all alone in strange rooms made me despair. Then it was that I had the daring—no, mad—idea of searching about in the surrounding countryside and imploring human charity. I inquired of the servants and found that there lived a kind and hospitable physician's family some few miles away—well, and here I sit now and am ashamed of my unprecedented boldness."

"There is really no reason for that. There is not the slightest reason for apologizing."

The stranger bowed to him to express a hearty feeling of gratitude.

"I then dare hope that you will permit me to trouble you for a few hours with my presence. As soon as the moon rises, the coachman has orders to hitch up the sleigh and transport me back again."

"You are most welcome to stay. It would give me great pleasure if our home could give you some compensation for your having missed your friends."

"Oh, that I am already quite sure of! But you will probably say that all this still does not explain why I am so anxious to be allowed to be incognito in your home. You may well call it a whim of mine, a childish fancy, a fixed idea. And nevertheless, my dear doctor, you will doubtless be able to understand that I—who am really seriously embarrassed by my inexcusable intrusion—shall be able to stand in a much freer relationship to you in that disguise."

Arnold found the idea rather extravagant but could think of nothing to say. His silence was taken for agreement and when the stranger—now quite cheerful—sank heavily back in his chair, he continued:

"Can you tell me, doctor—what satisfaction could you actually have if I introduced myself as Swindlefield, the wholesale merchant from Aarhus, or de Faultenberg, the architect from Copenhagen? I am, on the whole, of the opinion that the more that personal matters are withheld from conversation, the freer and more entertaining it becomes. Preconceptions at once establish a more or less restricted sphere of ideas which exerts the same influence on thought as the well-known chalk-circle about a hen. Isn't that right? Furthermore—it is carnival time, you know. We have almost a kind of duty to appear in disguise. The strict rules of everyday life are suspended for a short, happy time. Isn't that right?"

"Naturally," said Arnold with his embarrassed smile, "if that is what you wish. But we must call you *something*. We can't entirely dispense with a name or at least a title."

"Then call me—well, for example, call me Prince Carnival!"

They both began to laugh, Arnold half against his will. He felt uncertain about the man and at the same time oppressed by the other's social superiority.

Besides, he had with some uneasiness heard Emmy rustle about in the living room, the door to which stood ajar. She had lighted the lamp there, opened up the piano, and arranged the chairs in the proper order. Then she appeared suddenly in the door in her brown Sunday gown with a bow at her breast.

He observed at once that she had heard something of their conversation. Although the stranger bowed before her with the greatest courtesy and evinced pleasant surprise at her appearance, she remained standing in the doorway and returned his greeting with a very slight nod. At the same time she sent Arnold a glance out of the corner of her eye which as much as said, You should not have received him. Get rid of him!

He really wanted to follow her suggestion. But it was another thing to throw a good friend of Pastor Jørgensen out the door, particularly since there was nothing else to complain of in the man's behavior. And—as he had said—it *was* carnival time.

Arnold could think of nothing else to do but enter into the jest. With a somewhat threadbare attempt at humor, he said, "May I present to you a celebrated guest, H. R. H. Prince Carnival."

Emmy looked from the one to the other and did not conceal that she felt offended. She had actually heard most of what the stranger had said to Arnold, and through the maid she had further found out that he had brought with him two large suitcases which he had, without further ceremony, asked her to put in the guest room. Never had she seen the like of such impudence!

The stranger walked cheerfully toward her and repeated with many eloquent gestures his excuses and explanations. She looked at him suspiciously and did not answer; but he seemed so little to notice any bad feeling, that when Emmy after a few minutes silently retreated into the living room, the stranger gallantly escorted her.

Arnold followed, crestfallen. He too now thought that the jest had lasted long enough. But the man walked about smiling and expatiating on the comfort of the rooms, and apparently no longer thought that the slightest obligation rested upon him.

He stood near the piano; his eye had fallen on an old family portrait which hung on the wall. He spoke about its well-chosen colors, asked whom it represented, tried to guess the painter's name, and came upon the right name almost at once, although the picture was far from being the work of any master.

Could he be an artist? thought Arnold with surprise, and looked over at Emmy, who had emphatically placed herself in the corner of the sofa with her knitting.

The stranger was about to walk on when the piano suddenly captured his attention. "Oh, an old Marshall," he exclaimed delightedly. "Well, that is really interesting! In my childhood I learned to play my first exercises in five notes on this kind of instrument, and since then I have always loved its tone. Would you permit me to try it?"

Without waiting for permission, he seated himself on the piano stool, which groaned pitifully under the weight of his two to three hundred pounds. Emmy and Arnold looked helplessly at each other. Emmy's large owl eyes in particular were full of condemnation. What should they do with this mad being?

"The lady of the house plays, of course."

"My wife has had to give up her music," answered Arnold for her. "A housewife seldom has time on her hands."

"That is really a shame. The piano is a good one. It is only in need of use." He let his fingers run a few times over the keys and now began to play. It was a facetious Schubert minuet which Emmy had known note for note since she herself had practiced it with her music teacher. For this reason, she judged his playing purely professionally and was overwhelmed by his masterly technique and the delivery's bravura.

What she thought slipped unexpectedly from her tongue at the same moment that he finished. "You are a musician . . . a composer perhaps?" He rose, smiling, and bowed with his hand above his heart.

"My dear madam, I request most humbly that you believe me. I am really that which I represent myself to be. Of course—then you are acquainted with my illustrious family? My grandfather is the honorable Till Eulenspiegel. My father was named Tom Fool. And Harlequin is my cousin. My home is the land of milk and honey, and I am a commercial traveler dealing in the well-known roast squab which fly into the mouth of anyone who will yawn sufficiently."

Arnold joined in again with his brief and forced laughter. Emmy, on the other hand, remained quite unreceptive toward his witticisms. She regretted that she had spoken to him at all, sat there with her offended housewifely mien, and did not again lift her eyes from her knitting.

While he was playing, the boys had peered in curiously from the dining room, and the maid had finally understood a sign that she should take them away and put them to bed. Then the door was again quietly set ajar, but this time no one appeared.

"Are you acquainted with what I played, madam?" asked the stranger.

"Yes, it was Schubert's minuet," she answered in an indifferent tone. She could not help showing that she knew, but she was at the same time annoyed that she had again entered into conversation with him.

"Are you particularly fond of Schubert?" asked Arnold, and came nearer. He was quite without understanding for music but had the weakness of wanting to appear expert in all areas.

"Yes, I am very fond of Schubert. He has such a good-hearted humor. But my favorite composer at present is Petschoff. The gifted young Russian. You are acquainted with him, are you not?"

Emmy had never heard the name and was therefore silent. Arnold, however, asked, "Which compositions do you prize the most?"

The stranger thought for a moment and looked astutely at Arnold. Then he exclaimed with hands aloft: *The Dance of Death!* I can never hear the superb introductory bars without my heart beating wildly. I imagine that the trumpets sound like those which are to wake all us sleepers from the grave on the day of judgment."

The dining room door was finally opened completely. It was the middle-aged cook, who had been eavesdropping. Under the pretense of wanting to receive orders for supper, she shuffled in, hoping to get a better view of the stranger and an explanation of the peculiar goings on. From her corner of the sofa, Emmy motioned her away rather impatiently. But the cook did not let herself be sent away. She remained standing in the doorway with her large, jaundiced eyes rigidly and suspiciously fixed upon the strange man.

"Anna can go now," Emmy had to say finally. "I will come out and give instructions." Then Anna shuffled away, muttering under her breath.

"Wouldn't you like to play a little of the *Danse Macabre*?" Arnold asked.

"Oh, I am only a miserable amateur! But if you will be satisfied—." He seated himself again on the piano stool and by way of experiment made a run of chords, but then stopped, shook his head, and got up. While he remained standing with one hand on the piano, he cast a disquieted and almost self-conscious glance about the room.

"Yes, and now you certainly are again thinking that I am a queer fellow, but I have a request. Will you give me permission to light the candles in the chandelier? All of them! And then I must request permission to change my clothes.—I was so free a few moments ago as to have my baggage brought to your guest room. As I said before, I am only an amateur, and it is quite impossible for me to enter into the right mood for music without being in full dress."

Both Emmy and Arnold gave a visible start. They again involuntarily looked at each other. Now they no longer were in doubt that the man had a screw loose.

He walked across the floor and began calmly to explain. Petschoff's music, he said, had affected him in about the same way that Shakespeare's poetry had affected one of his friends, who for a long time had not been able to evolve any interest for Shakespeare. That friend had once been advised to attire himself in formal clothes some evening and decorate his apartment with flowers and lights as if he were expecting highly honored guests, and only then to begin to read "As You Like It" in the hours either side of midnight. He had followed the advice and had since admitted that not only Shakespeare's world but the world of poetry had been revealed to him that night in all its magnificence.

"And so it goes, no doubt, with most of us poor mortals in regard to the arts. And perhaps with life on the whole. Unless one has something of the devil within one, one understands nothing of the work of a genius. Nor of the Creator. This I have had—as I said before —to realize, particularly with respect to Petschoff's music.'

Now he stepped in front of Emmy and said, with his head inclined in a pleading manner, "Would you be greatly offended, madam, if I reminded you of the loveliest Mediterranean blue or Himalaya-colored silk gown which you, without doubt, have hanging someplace or other in the gloom of a wardrobe, where it only affords pleasure to moths and other creatures of darkness? And you, honored doctor, would you seriously object to dressing yourself in your formal clothes on the occasion of this celebration of Petschoff's revival? Indeed, would you permit me with all propriety to turn things somewhat upside down here in your house this evening? It is carnival time! And I have told you who I am. You should therefore not be provoked with me."

His clear, light brown eyes, which bore a vague resemblance to the eyes of a goat, peered first at the one and then at the other with a questioning and urgent glance. Because neither of them answered, he took leave of them, while he—bowing respectfully—expressed the hope that he was in possession of a little of that gift of persuasion one ascribes to a certain person about whom it is said, "If one offers him a finger, et cetera, et cetera . . .

While still in the doorway, he bowed twice and said, smiling, "Until we meet again!"

No sooner had he left than Emmy flew up from the sofa, threw her knitting to one side, and hastened to her husband. "This is terrible! What shall we do? He is certainly mad!"

"Yes, he is obviously not quite all there."

"Who do you think he can be?"

"Indeed, I don't know. But I can remember that Pastor Jørgensen once mentioned one of his friends—a large landowner I believe—who fell from a wagon during some student festivity and afterward became rather queer."

"You should not have received him. That was not right." She said this with an expression which made him smile out of tenderness because it reminded him in a moving way of her nervous girlhood days when she had been frightened by everything and immediately sought refuge in his protection.

"I believe he's frightened you," he said, and put his arm about her. "Your heart is actually pounding."

"Yes, but—will you tell me—what shall we do?"

"Oh, we should only treat him with all possible kindness. Above all, we must not give the pastor any reason to complain that his guest was not received properly. You go out and make arrangements in the kitchen. We can now put all our good food to use in the bargain. Let's have both red wine and sherry on the table, since we already have it here in the house."

"Yes, but you yourself think the man is crazy."

"Well . . . crazy . . . that's perhaps an overstatement. Perhaps he has water on the brain and that's the whole of it. Incidentally, he really made a very pleasant impression, it seems to me, and he's quite entertaining. And now he wants to play for us. What was the name of that Russian?"

Emmy answered distractedly. With her hands on Arnold's shoulders, she pressed her soft body tightly against him as if in fear, but her thoughts were far away.

Arnold continued to reassure her. "He really plays very well indeed. He showed surprising skill. It may be very pleasant to have a little music festival. We haven't enjoyed much of that sort of thing during the last few years."

Emmy had got a hold of the top button of his vest, which was visible at the neck of his housecoat.

"But you can't mean that, Arnold—you don't seriously want me, as he said, to put on my pink silk dress?"

Arnold started to laugh. "No, that I really don't! . . . Although, after all, why not? I wouldn't at all object to seeing you in your finery once more. You haven't had it on since your uncle's big party—can you remember? And Lord, it *is* carnival time.—Yes, look at me. But I mean it in all seriousness!"

"Oh, you can't be, Arnold! That would be idiotic . . . completely insane!" She shook him hard by the button of his vest, and her face became redder and redder. Arnold became enthusiastic about seeing her decked out. He threw his other arm around her and tried to steal a kiss. "I tell you I am serious! I really want to have a lark for once. Do you hear, Emmy! I want to see you in your silk dress. I want to see you in all your magnificence!"

"No, no—there's no use, Arnold! That will never do. Remember, I am an old woman!—What would the maids say?"

"The maids?"

"Yes. Tomorrow the whole town would be talking about it."

This prophecy cooled his ardor for a moment. In his mind's eye he saw Sørensen the schoolteacher tottering about with a malicious smile, regaling others with the news. But, on the other hand, that vision stimulated him the more.

"Let people talk! What does it matter to us? Anyway, it is a good old established custom to have a little fun during carnival time.—Come on! Now we shall both go in and put on our Sunday best."

"No, Arnold. I won't do it. The dress doesn't fit me anymore."

"What of it? We are not going into high society."

"And it's so low cut."

"Yes, and what of it? You are at your loveliest in the white silk costume the Creator himself sewed for you. —Ouch!"

She had given him a slap on the ear.

"Will monsieur behave!"

He laughed and threw both arms wildly around her legs in order to carry her away.

"This is insane! Arnold! . . . Arnold!" She continued to cry while she struggled—and let herself be dragged toward the bedroom door. "Are you two men equally mad?"

Suddenly he released her, and they rushed away from each other. The dining room door had squeaked. It was old Anna, who again shuffled in in her carpet slippers to ask about supper. She had evidently heard something, for she remained standing in the doorway and stared, bewildered, with her ugly, open mouth.

Arnold got angry and hastened toward her in order to scold her, but Emmy placed herself between them and gave the cook instructions with her usual firmness and housewifely presence of mind. The duck, she said, should be served cold together with the salads, and cream should be whipped for the prune tarts. The butter should be fixed in balls, and the cheese should be cubed and arranged on a fancy napkin—

"We are going to celebrate tonight!" interrupted Arnold with forced liveliness. "Have you forgotten that it's carnival time, Anna?"

III

On a starry autumn evening six and a half years ago when Arnold and Emmy had come as newlyweds to Sønderbøl they had arrived by stagecoach, and their abundant baggage had had to be unloaded in great haste on the highway in front of the house, among the heap of trunks and goods, there had been a brand new wicker traveling case which Emmy had watched with special anxiety and had carried into safety right away.

It was that case which she opened first the next day when she began to unpack and put things away in her new home. It contained the treasures of her unmarried years, first and foremost, keepsakes from her wedding: the bridal gown, the veil, and the myrtle wreath, besides the bouquet that Arnold had sent her before the ceremony, the music and the printed songs, Arnold's letters and small gifts from the time of their engagement; and, finally, the most valuable items of her trousseau, among them a pink silk dress with white lace trim, which she had worn to a family gathering the day before the wedding.

In the first year, she had often resorted to occupying herself with these treasures in the long, empty, and lonesome hours when Arnold was away. She would sit then on the edge of the open drawer and let the moods which had accompanied the wedding pass through her mind. Or she would try on her pretty dresses in front of the mirror, do her hair up with jewelry and flowers, and behave in a fashion which she had since smiled at and found affected. As she was accustomed to say, she had, thank goodness, found something else to think of and something else to expend her energy upon. She could still remember—yes, almost feel—how her thoughts during the course of her first pregnancy slowly turned from the past toward the future. Year after year, new drawers had to be found in chests and closets in order to create room for children's clothing.

Since she planned now to wear her silk dress, she had to look in an old cardboard box which stood uppermost in the clothespress; and when she saw the dress, she immediately gave up the thought of wearing it and proclaimed that she would not be a party to this foolishness.

Arnold's courage was also rapidly evaporating. The mere removal of his housecoat and the necessity of bringing forth his formal clothes sobered him. But now it would be too embarrassing to give up the fun. In order to give himself courage, he began to chide Emmy. She must not be silly! Even if the dress was a little wrinkled and also perhaps a little old-fashioned in its cut—what did that matter? The whole affair was only a carnival jest.

Emmy would not listen. She seated herself on the edge of the bed and, on the verge of tears, repeated vehemently that she would not make a fool of herself.

At the same time, out in the kitchen, a moving scene was taking place.

Old Anna was pattering about in her carpet slippers and grumbling, as was her custom when something failed to go according to her established routine. She had just come up from the cellar with the cold duck on a plate and had given the younger maid orders to put a pan on the stove when the stranger suddenly appeared in the doorway in full dress with a rose in his buttonhole.

She sank to one knee and groaned. She nearly dropped the plate. She could not have been more agitated if it had been the devil himself who had appeared behind her.

He remained standing in the doorway and nodded pleasantly to her. "Don't let me disturb you! I only wanted to say . . . I see that you have begun to set the table in the dining room; but it is rather cold in there and not really cozy. I would suggest that you set the table in the living room. You can then use the dining room as a pantry."

Anna set the plate down on the kitchen table with such force that the plate rang.

"I ain't taking orders from others than the doctor and Missus—I'd like to have you know."

He looked at her firmly for a moment.

"It is not a matter of orders," he said then in an unchanged, friendly tone. "It is only a suggestion. But I am, for that matter, quite sure that your mistress would assent to it. Kindly have the goodness to do what I say. And if you should by chance have access to any fine old silverware or any beautiful porcelain—a vase or something similar—would you please bring that forth."

"I don't know what's happening here," said the cook, almost in tears because of her own ill temper and growing fear.—"You can have it! I ain't going to have nothing more to do with it!"

She tore off her apron and threw it down on a kitchen chair, stumbled into the maid's room, and slammed the door behind her.

The stranger shrugged his shoulders.

He then motioned to the younger maid, who had tried to conceal herself in the corner next to the stove. She was a child of fifteen, a little, red-cheeked, fair-haired girl with a pair of large, ethereal blue, simple, happy eyes.

"Come here, my little friend!" he said.

She obeyed as if hypnotized. Cheerfully she placed herself before him, with her face upturned, her arms dangling, just like a schoolchild before its teacher.

"Come on with me. We two must help each other set the table. But that must be done in silence. No noise!—Let me see, what do you have on your feet?"

She stretched her right foot forward as if at a command to show that she was in her stocking feet.

"That's all right! But no talking either! Remember that! It's to be a surprise, you understand.—Wait a moment! What is your name?"

"Abelone."

He patted her cheek.

"That's a good name. A festive name. But listen now, my little friend! You certainly have another dress to put on beside this old washrag? A black dress, haven't you? Your confirmation dress? And a clean white apron?—Good! Come along!"

In the living room, he had already made the first preparations in silence. He had moved the commonplace rows of potted plants away from the windowsills and had carefully arranged them as decorations around the room. The round table had been rolled away from the sofa and placed in the middle of the floor under the chandelier, and Abelone was told to set the table here.

At first, everything seemed hopeless. She was as obedient as an automaton but, to be sure, one which is incorrectly adjusted. She continually misunderstood his directions because, with the bedroom so close, he did not dare speak, but had to be satisfied with signs and gestures. When she was directed to procure wine glasses, she went to the kitchen with great agility but returned with the dust mop; and when he wanted a vase, she came back bearing a pail.

Suddenly a door creaked. Quick steps were heard in the hall to the bedroom. He was startled. But the steps flew past and disappeared.

It was Arnold, in shirt sleeves, with a lamp in his hand. He was on his way up to one of the attic storage rooms, where his dress coat hung. He was humming as he went, but was in reality in a terrible humor. Inwardly he had an uncomfortable sensation of embarrassment and wished that the parasitic stranger and his carnival jest would go to the devil.

Up in the darkness and loneliness of the attic he regained his reason. With a feeling of relief at being freed from an unpleasant delusion, he realized that Emmy was right in that they both stood helplessly on the verge of making fools of themselves. He left the dress coat where it was and went quickly and resolutely down the stairs.

But he was no longer capable of stopping the course of fate. When he returned to the bedroom, he was received with an unexpected sight which again set his mind ablaze. Emmy had finally not been able to resist the charm of the pink silk. During his absence, she had tried on the dress by way of experiment and was now standing in front of the mirror and stretching by standing on the tips of her toes in order to be thin enough about the waist so that she could hook her belt.

"Really!" He stretched out both arms.—"Emmy! You are wonderful!"

She could hardly hook her belt from nervousness. Her cheeks blushed wildly. She had been afraid that he would find her ridiculous and begin to laugh. Her heart had begun to pound noticeably when she heard him come back through the hall.

"Do you think it is still becoming to me?"

"Splendid, dear! Absolutely grand! And it fits you very well indeed. To think that you haven't changed more than that!"

"Do you think I should put this on too?" From a red box she took two silver oak leaves with small diamond dew drops. Together they formed a diadem. Arnold stood behind her and looked over her head into the mirror while she fastened the jewelry in her hair.

"Do you remember it?" she asked.

"Do I! . . . Think how long ago!"

"Do you think I should wear it?"

"Superb! Absolutely splendid! You become a fairy princess! . . . I tell you Emmy, you have never been lovelier!"

She blushed again. And in a sudden burst of exuberant happiness, she leaned over backwards, put both arms around his head, and pressed her lips against his.

"Once more!" he said, laughing.

At the same moment, a hand touched the piano keys in the living room.

They released each other in surprise. They both had almost forgotten their strange guest.

"That's frightful," said Emmy. "He is already there."

"Never mind! Now he is amusing himself by playing," said Arnold consolingly.

To the tones of a magnificent festive march they completed their dressing. But Arnold had, of course, to go to the attic once more, and furthermore, he continually had to give Emmy assistance, yes, even once use needle and thread in order to make the dress fit. All this delayed them so much more, since it at once became the occasion for a renewed exchange of kisses and other kinds of playfulness, just as if they were on their honeymoon.

Arm in arm they took one last review of themselves before the mirror. But in the doorway into the parlor they had once more to overcome their embarrassment. With somewhat forced laughter, one tried to get the other to go in first, until Arnold suddenly threw open the door and rushed in with Emmy on his arm.

Then they both stiffened like a couple of pillars and their laughter changed into an expression of amazement. They did not recognize their own parlor. Lights were burning not only in the chandelier in the ceiling but also in several wall lamps which had not been used since the banquet when their first child was baptized. And there were flowers everywhere. In the middle of the table stood a large bowl full of lovely yellow roses between which there peeped out ripe peaches and bunches of blue grapes. Across the tablecloth were spread small bouquets of violets.

The stranger had risen from the piano. With his hand on his heart he greeted them respectfully.

"Gracious madam! Honored doctor! You will, I hope, forgive me for having, quite unasked, elevated myself to master of ceremonies at this little improvised festivity. I also ask forgiveness for having allowed myself to use a little table decoration which I brought along in my trunk in order not to come quite empty-handed to my old friend the pastor. As you see, it will not stand being kept."

Emmy and Arnold had stopped feeling surprise at anything. While Emmy went around the table with an expression like that of a child around a Christmas tree, Arnold remained standing at the door with his arms at his side and let his dazzled eyes run over the entire room.

Finally he went to his guest and pressed his hand.

"Your royal highness!" he said with a bow—and there was no longer anything awkward in his gaiety. "May I request you to be so kind as to escort my wife to the supper table!"

IV

They had now been sitting at the table for nearly an hour and had reached the dessert course. Little red-cheeked Abelone, who attended to waiting on the table, looked very pretty in her black confirmation dress and her white apron; but her service was something both to laugh and cry about. Once she tripped over the long dress, sending several plates flying across the floor. And to her utter confusion, neither the doctor nor her mistress became angry about it or reproached her. The doctor even began to laugh and exclaimed, "Da capo!"

Old Anna stood eavesdropping outside the half-open dining room door. In the end, curiosity had gotten the better of her. She had finally even lent a hand in setting the table, but now she was again quite beside herself with annoyance at what she was witness to.

It was the stranger who did the talking. Arnold could hardly do anything but laugh. He had after a time given up trying to discover who the stranger was. He no longer cared to know. For better or for worse, he abandoned himself to the adventurous mood of the moment.

Emmy did not, however, feel quite sure of herself and was on her guard. The stranger's anecdotes became at times rather bold. But despite all his talkativeness, he did not seem in any way presumptuous or noisy. In contrast with Arnold, who was becoming somewhat befuddled, he did not seem particularly affected by the wine. The color in his cheeks had become only a trifle deeper, and the roguishness in his clear, goat-like eyes had, as it were, ventured a little farther out into the light. He resembled an aging satyr as he sat there and smiled with his wine-red mouth while the graying brown locks of hair stood up about his shiny pate like an autumnal wreath of vine leaves.

Emmy had not forgotten his promise to play for them. When the dessert plates had been brought on and Abelone finally could be dispensed with, she reminded him of it. He made no objection, but solicited a favor before he began. He asked for permission, as he said, to crown her most humbly as queen of the festival. She did not understand what he meant, and she did not feel herself quite as courageous with this new caprice as she had before. But as usual, when she did not answer right away, he took her silence for consent. He had already plundered the fruit bowl of some of the largest and most beautiful roses, and these he now secured with a light and dexterous hand in her hair so that they formed a wreath under the silver diadem.

At first she did not like it. It was uncomfortable to have his heavy body so near to her and to feel his fingers in her hair. She was also afraid that Abelone might come in. But after having mirrored herself in the looks of the two men and seen that the coronation costume became her, she no longer offered any resistance. Arnold was completely swept away with admiration. He clapped his hands and cried out unrestrainedly how wonderful she was.

"And now music!" she said peremptorily, caught up in her role as queen.

The stranger bowed deeply before her:

"I am your majesty's most humble servant!"

But instead of going to the piano, he disappeared through Arnold's room to the vestibule and came back with a long-necked instrument inlaid with mother-of-pearl—a cross between a mandolin and a lute. Emmy was a little disappointed. Arnold, on the other hand, cried bravo.

"Your royal highness is also a singer!" he said.

"In a very modest and inoffensive way!"

First he sang a French and then two amorous Italian folk songs.

Arnold, who understood but little of the text, and who did not enjoy music, soon became inattentive. He leaned against the back of the chair and, smiling, fingered his mustache while he looked at Emmy with a glance which was moist with wine and love. He began now to have enough of the strange man. He longed again to be alone with Emmy. They would continue the party entirely for themselves and in still bolder ways. The maids should be sent to bed as quickly as possible. Only the burning lights should be witness to their oriental, nocturnal festival.

The stranger had begun a new song, this time a Danish one. It was a song about the god of adventure who traveled about incognito in the world in cap and bells and lured sleepy cupids and melancholy satyrs out of gloomy lofts and dark cellars, where the boredom of everyday life had chased them and caused them to become moldy. The melody was gay and full of humor, and every stanza ended with a refrain of six lines:

> And life goes on its stumbling way,
> Turns wrong to right,
> Turns night to day,
> Turns inside out and upside down,
> Hurra, hurra, here comes the clown,
> Once more to set the world aright.

Arnold had not been able to take his moist eyes away from Emmy, who was listening with her hand under her chin. He sat and thought that she was not particularly attentive either, but that she, like himself, only longed to be relieved of this inconvenient guest. There was something of a love-dreaming maenad about her as she sat there with her bare elbow on the table and her hand at her flower-decked throat. Her eyelids sank. About her mouth lay a fixed, secretive, smile.

He tried to attract her attention by jostling her a bit under the table with the toe of his shoe. He found her foot; but in spite of the fact that he finally pushed rather forcibly, she did not look up. Then he slowly withdrew his foot and became suspicious.

Shortly thereafter, when the song was finished, the stranger stood up with his glass in his hand and proposed a toast to the cloven-footed retainers of the god of adventure, to all the little spirits who stole away hearts, dulled the wits, and disturbed the sleep, and who in nature's royal household fulfilled a purpose similar to that of certain molds in fine champagne: they gave that drink of life its bouquet and made it sparkle.

He bowed before Emmy and, as in a dream, she lifted up her glass to his with a gleaming and enraptured expression which sobered Arnold completely.

The stranger now also turned to him.

"Your health, doctor! A toast to depravity! For the aroma of life and death!"

Arnold did not touch his glass and looked stiffly ahead as though he had not heard anything.

"But what is the matter with you?" asked Emmy reproachfully. "Won't you touch glasses with us?"

He had put both hands in his pockets and did not answer.

For a moment it was unpleasantly still. Then the stranger took out his large gold watch and said that he unfortunately would now have to break up the party. The hour was much too late. His coachman must have fallen asleep over at the inn and have forgotten the time. They rose in silence, Emmy with an annoyed and ashamed air—and the guest made his farewells. When Arnold wanted to follow him outside, the stranger tried to prevent it.

"Don't trouble yourself, my dear doctor. It is cold out there in the hall, and you have observed that I can shift for myself very well."

But Arnold had already become more calm and wished to fulfill his obligations to the end. When they came to the vestibule, he offered to send over to the inn for the sleigh, to which the stranger, however, objected most firmly.

"I should say not; you are not going to have that trouble on my account. You see here"—he pointed to his large, fur-lined overshoes and laughed—"I'll be over there in a moment. These are the famous seven league boots, you understand."

The parting was short and on Arnold's side marked by cold politeness. It was as if he had to prevail upon himself to ask the stranger to give Pastor Jørgensen his regards.

When he came into his room, Emmy was standing there. She had placed herself behind the rocking chair and was waiting agitatedly for an explanation. She had closed the door to the living room so that the maids who were cleaning off the table there should not hear anything.

But Arnold went past her without speaking a word. He went through the living room into the bedroom in order to put on his housecoat. When, on his way back, he noticed that the candles were still burning, both in the chandelier and on the walls, his anger got the better of him.

"Put out the candles, damn it!" he bellowed. "Are you absolutely crazy! Put them out, I say!"

When he got back to his room, Emmy was still standing in the same place. She had at first supposed his behavior at the table to be the result of intoxication and was really ashamed of him. There was something within her—a little uneasiness in her conscience—which told her that there must be something else wrong.

There was no real firmness in the offended tone with which she now asked what all this meant.

He turned his head toward her as if he had just noticed her and measured her slowly from top to toe.

"You heard it! I said that they should put out the lights in there. There is certainly no point in letting the lights burn all night."

He had brought in a table lamp from the other room. He sat down at his writing desk and opened up his record book as if to put time to good advantage by writing out some bills.

Emmy stood with her arms on the back of the chair. She leaned forward and began to rock back and forth. As uneasy as she was, she could hardly suppress a smile. It wakened so many gay memories for her to see him thus. She had almost forgotten how handsome he could look when he was thoroughly angry with her.

She also remembered now how she used to placate him when he felt himself slighted by her or others. After having given him time enough to collect himself, she went to him and seated herself bravely on the arm of the chair. With her arm about his head she said:

"Arnold—have I done something wrong?"

The effect was quite different from what it had been during their engagement. He pushed her away harshly asked to be relieved of her proximity.

"But Arnold—!"

Now she was offended in earnest and scolded him well. He thereupon turned toward her with an expression so distorted that she was involuntarily silenced.

"Surely you can see that I am busy. Now you have amused yourself quite sufficiently for this evening."— And he added, while he measured her a few times with a contemptuous glance: "You doubtless need very much to get some rest. You are very overwrought. The stranger has certainly not had a beneficial influence on your nervous system."

She raised her head suddenly and looked at him with surprise and distress. She expected that he would take back his last words. When he did not, she said in a low voice as she turned her back upon him:

"You ought to be ashamed!"

After a moment she went out of the room.

When she entered the bedroom and stood in front of the mirror, she suddenly blushed at herself and her half-nakedness. She threw a light dressing gown about her and shamefacedly plucked the roses from her hair.

But she lingered as she did so and had a hidden sympathy for herself, like one who must take leave of an all too beautiful dream. Then she went into the adjacent nursery to take a look at the children, gave the maids some last instructions through the door into the kitchen hallway, locked the door, and went back to the bedroom.

There the two beds stood peacefully side by side at right angles to the wall, their blankets turned down. Close to the ceiling burned a hanging lamp with a pink shade. She had herself lighted it while she was dressing; it had otherwise not been used for many years. Now she pulled it down and extinguished it.

She then seated herself dejectedly in front of the mirror and began to loosen her hair. She was no longer angry with Arnold, although she did not understand how he could have had the heart to ruin the pleasure of this evening for the both of them. But she should have foreseen it. She knew from other days how unreasonable he could be, and thus was able to forgive him. When he had had a night's sleep, he would himself realize how laughable his suspicion had been and would regret it.

She undressed slowly and went to bed—although she let the light burn for some time longer. It was a whole hour before she heard Arnold come in. Then she pretended that she was asleep.

V

The next morning they were still unreconciled. Emmy had had her hands full all morning, bringing the house into order after the disturbance of the previous day, and, in addition, a noisy argument between the maids had broken out over a twenty-crown gold piece which the stranger had left on the washstand in the guest room. Old Anna, who had her own secret misgivings about the strange male being, and who still smelled sulphur in the rooms, did not dare take her part of the money but, on the other hand, begrudged Abelone every single bit more than the third rightfully due her. In this painful situation she was more ill-natured than usual and Emmy had to go out into the kitchen time after time and make peace.

Arnold had been called out to a tenant farmer's family far out on the heath and could not be expected home before late afternoon. When Emmy finally was through with her housework and while the children took their nap after dinner, she began, as on other days, to feel lonesome and to long for his return. She was accustomed to use this undisturbed hour on her household accounts, but today she did not have the composure for that kind of work. It was the first time in their married life that there had been such serious and prolonged bad feeling between them. Arnold had not even said good morning to her and had left without saying goodbye. She finally sat down at the window in his room, from where she could watch the highway, with its telegraph poles, that led all the way out to the hills of the heath. She sat with the darning in her hand and a basket of woolens in front of her and now and then cast a searching glance up the highway.

It was thawing, a still, gray day with lowering clouds. The lifeless weather exercised an especially depressing influence here, where one was used to hearing the west wind sough or a southeaster sweep past the house like an affectionate cat mewing at the doors and the windows. A sleepy dripping from the eaves was all that relieved the heavy silence.

Occasionally people walked past in the slush; but contrary to her wont, she did not notice who they were. Even when she saw Sørensen the schoolteacher striding across the road on his tottering, knock-kneed legs, his form, together with a fleeting conjecture that he was again concerned with that petition, passed through her consciousness like a shadow.

She sat and thought of something that she wanted to say to Arnold when he finally had repented and had begged her pardon. She actually wanted him no different from what he was. But she would take her lord and master by his ear and let him know that he did not have the right to suspect her of having such bad taste that she would prefer a middle-aged and bald musician with cherub cheeks to a man like him. Perhaps she would also remind him of the time while they were engaged when he had sent back her ring simply because she had danced two dances with someone else at a fraternity dance and had allowed herself to be treated to an ice cream cone. Arnold had often talked about that himself in Sønderbøl and had cursed himself for his folly.

But she also thought of him, the stranger, while she sat there at the window and watched. She tried to think of some way to get in touch with the parsonage so that they could find out who he was. How difficult it was for her to grasp that he still existed and actually was not so far away that he couldn't, for that matter, appear bodily at the door. The evening's experiences had already faded like something she had only dreamed; and, after all, that was the way she preferred to imagine them.

It was late in the afternoon before Arnold came home. The children had long since risen from their naps. Emmy had sat down in the living room with the boys and was showing them pictures.

Her heart flew into her throat when she heard him in the vestibule. While she distractedly answered the boys' questions, she listened to his steps, and she seemed to be able to perceive that he was in a more conciliatory mood.

He did greet her when he came in and asked—although a little curtly—about his dinner. She wondered for a moment whether she should follow him into the dining room, but she remained seated and sent the older boy into the kitchen with instructions to the maids. It was really his place to take the first step!

When Arnold had eaten, he came in again, with the obvious design of making advances. For the present, the children would have to serve as a bridge between them. He patted them on their heads, asked what sort of pictures they had been looking at and what they had amused themselves with during the day. Finally Emmy joined in the conversation with a few words which seemed casually dropped.

With the mere sound of her voice—quiet and uncertain as it was—the last dregs of bitterness were dissolved in his mind. A little while later, when the boys were called in to their afternoon sandwiches and they were alone, he went over to her and laid his hands on her head.

"Shall we let the whole thing be forgotten, Emmy?"

In answer, she lifted a pair of tear-filled eyes and a tightly closed mouth toward him. Her lips spread and trembled like those of an unjustly treated child who fights against tears.

"Now, now! No more scenes!" he admonished her softly and got her—as in the sealing of a peace pact—to smile.

About the events of the previous evening not a word was spoken; indeed, they did not have an opportunity to talk more together. Even before Arnold was through with his coffee, another wagon stopped outside the door.

Contrary to custom, Emmy followed him all the way out to the cold vestibule and took great pains to see that he was well wrapped up. When he came back that evening, she had already sent the maids to bed, and she stood in the doorway with a light in order to help him off with his wraps.

But the serpent had slipped into their little paradise. The next day, when Arnold was walking home in the twilight after having made a call in town, he was startled to hear someone playing in the parlor. As he stood and listened, his pulse became more rapid. Could it be possible? . . . Could it be *he*?

The door to the living room was closed; but by the fumbling delivery, he gradually realized that it was Emmy herself who was playing. He now recognized one of the languishing French or Italian melodies which the stranger had sung.

He opened the door suddenly and went in. She had apparently not heard him come. He had really succeeded in surprising her, and he could see that her thoughts had been astray. She stopped playing immediately. As she got up, she quickly glanced up at him obliquely with a shy and searching look in her eyes.

Without saying a word, he went into the bedroom and put on his housecoat. When he came back, she was standing at the window and looking out. Turning to him, she asked if he wanted the lamp lighted. He answered no.

"That's something new, to see you at the piano," he said from the armchair in the corner by the stove after a brief silence. "What was that you were playing?"

"Oh—only some finger exercises."

It pained her to have to lie to him. It was the first time she had done so in many years, but she did not know what else to answer. She knew how hopeless it would be to try to explain her feelings to him. Indeed, she did not really understand them herself. She could not express what it was that made her so melancholy. And how does one find the word that really explains such lonely thoughts, thoughts which hover about the strange and forbidden, "that bit of hereditary depravity," that eternal longing which, he had said, preserves a woman's love so sparkling and fresh and confers upon it its sweetness?

Arnold's continued silence ultimately made her apprehensive. The children's glad voices, audible from the dining room, only augmented her anxiety. It was as if with every minute's silence, miles separated her from the other members of her family. It seemed to her that more and more they were disappearing into an immense abyss of darkness and cold. She knew that she had erred. With horror she stared down into the depths of her own heart, down into the hidden and unsuspected abysses where demons beckoned.

She turned around dizzily and her fearful eyes sought Arnold. He sat slouched in the armchair, with a face so pale that it glimmered in the twilight.

She clasped her bosom, went to him, and fearfully laid her hand on his shoulder.

"Arnold–"

She got no farther. He grasped her arm and flung it from him with such a brutal strength that she fell to the floor.

"Hussy!" he hissed.

She had fallen on her side in the middle of the floor. Confused by his sudden, violent reaction, hurt by anger and shame, and filled with a sensual pleasure which inspired her with new, paralyzing terror, she remained on her knees with her face in her hands. Not until after almost a minute was she able to rise. Slowly she went into the bedroom, still concealing her face in her hands.

VI

Two days later Arnold came driving over the heath with a western storm at his back. He was leaning back in his seat and had pulled his fur coat well up above his ears. There was not much to be seen of him besides his beard and a pair of gray wool mittens. The heavy, wood pipe which customarily connected hand and mouth like a handle was gone today; neglected, it hung with its stem down in the side pocket of the carriage.

He had not spoken to Emmy for a day and a half now. Out of respect for the children and the servants, they had sat together during meals and had avoided every rupture in the household's daily life. But after meals they went their separate ways. Since the first evening, when Emmy had lain in bed and wept and called softly to him, she had likewise not made the slightest attempt at reconciliation.

What he felt toward her was really no longer anger but more nearly pity. He excused her because she was a woman, a being with an abnormal emotional life and, consequently, fluid, confused reasoning. He was not even sure that she had not begun to view herself as unjustly treated. There was something in the defiance which she had lately shown toward him which might point to that. And that would be just like her! He remembered from former days how she, in the most innocent fashion, could continue with her denials until she herself believed them, even when he had quantities of proof against her on hand!

He tried to blame only himself for the disappointment he had suffered. As he constantly said to himself, he had not been a hair's breadth better than most loving husbands, whose blindness he so often had joined in deriding in the theater and in reality. He had created an ideal picture of his wife and now that the halo had disappeared, he was forced to realize the truth of the saying that there was at the bottom of even the most innocent woman's heart a poisonous viper lying dormant. Only chance determined whether it was left to doze or was awakened to bring ruin.

He had been to an inquest at the house of a poor tenant farmer out on the heath and was now on his way home. He customarily took a little nap while driving across the desolate tract of land, where one seldom met anyone; but even sleep forsook him this time. Nor did he feel any desire to count the telegraph poles or to add long numbers in his head in order to ward off boredom. Just as life had turned a strange countenance toward him, so nature had renewed itself for him in these days. The great, bleak landscape and the vast, cloudy sky drew forth his thoughts with a power he had long not felt. While he sat there enveloped by the storm, there were reborn in his mind pregnant and solemn moods which moved the heart and made fruitful his thoughts.

He had half begun to adjust himself and feel content in his loneliness, which he viewed as irremediable. There were moments when he was near to regarding the floundering of his happiness as a kind of liberation, or when he at least found compensation for it in that sadness of renunciation which opens the mind toward eternity.

The thought of the strange man was the thorn in his flesh which never let him forget his humiliation for long. Until he knew for certain that the stranger had left the region, he would have no peace. Although he had to admit that he had nothing of consequence to reproach *him* with, Arnold's feelings toward the stranger were of such a kind that another meeting might prove fateful.

The carriage had now rolled over the farthest hills of the heath. At a quick trot it now approached the village of Sønderbøl. There the village, with its mill, the chimney of its cooperative creamery, and the doctor's own red house, lay spread out upon the snow-patched fields, just as he had seen it from the slope of the hill hundreds of times before—and yet so completely changed. Today there bubbled up within him no cozy feeling of happiness at the sight of his home. His paradise had disappeared into the earth, and in its place lay this disconsolate collection of houses on the windy plain—a piece of denuded reality intensely melancholy and wretched, but also solemnly great in its wild nakedness.

When he neared the first house in the town, his carriage was halted by a tall, white-haired farmer who wished to speak with him.

It was the same Thorvald Andersen whom Emmy a few days previous had seen going into the schoolteacher's house with a piece of paper in his hand. Therefore, he surmised at once that Andersen wanted to talk to him about this petition. The man was devoted to him because Arnold once had helped his wife during a serious illness. Besides, the farmer was continuously at odds with Sørensen the schoolteacher because of some school fines. Nevertheless, he was always very doubtful about taking Arnold's side against the schoolteacher. The schoolteacher was born of a farmer's family and therefore belonged to Andersen's own class, and although the populace shared neither the schoolteacher's religious belief nor his political conviction, they secretly admired him because of his great shrewdness and his ability to find his way to the opposition's most sensitive point under the guise of friendship.

Arnold understood immediately from the expression on the farmer's face that he had a confession to make. He almost had to laugh at the man's embarrassment. The whole matter had become so thoroughly one of indifference to him.

The man began by excusing himself for detaining him while Arnold had visitors waiting for him at home.

"Visitors?" asked Arnold.

Yes, a short time ago he had seen Pastor Jørgensen's closed wagon drive through the village.

In order not to betray himself, Arnold drew forth his handkerchief and blew his nose repeatedly. For a few minutes he endured listening to the man's stammering explanation. Then he cut him off curtly and gave the coachman orders to drive on.

He did indeed find visitors in the living room when he reached home. Pastor Jørgensen was rushing about with flying coattails. His wife with her hat on was sitting on the sofa behind the table. Arnold barely noticed them. He cast his eye toward Emmy, who sat in an armchair near the pastor's wife, without really seeing her. His glance flitted about seeking one who was not there.

Emmy had been on guard from the moment she heard him coming, in order to observe his expression the moment he strode in. It was with triumph that she saw jealousy burning in his searching eyes.

Pastor Jørgensen placed himself before Arnold and grasped his lapels with both hands as if he wanted to dance with him. He was one of those people who, even in the homes of others, must constantly wander about, and who continually looks at his watch with fright and explains that now he must be leaving, and whom one nevertheless cannot get rid of. He stood and told Arnold what he already had explained to Emmy, that he and his wife wanted them to come to dinner the following Sunday, together with several other inhabitants of the district. They had preferred, he said, to bring them the invitation in person but, as it happened, could only stay a moment. Arnold thanked him for the invitation in a way which could be taken for either yes or no.

Wine and cake was now brought in. The pastor complained to Arnold about the arthritis in his shoulder, and his wife told Emmy about her maids. Neither of them had as yet said a word about their strange friend.

Arnold sat there silent, boiling with excitement. What he had feared the most had happened. The humiliation which he and the whole family had undergone had been disclosed by the stranger, and, in the interests of delicacy, the pastor and his wife did not even mention the stranger's visit.

He did not know where he should turn his eyes. He was especially afraid of meeting Emmy's glance. Had he been alone with her, he would have struck her to the ground again. A voice shrieked within him: Your name a matter of scandal! Your home sacrificed to gossip! Your future ruined!

All right! Everything else might as well be lost too! Now they should speak their minds!

In order to force the pastor to talk about the stranger, Arnold thought of a stratagem. He turned the conversation again to Pastor Jørgensen's arthritis and said that it had probably flared up during his excursion a few days before in the heavy snowstorm.

The pastor did not understand him. He had certainly not been out in any snowy weather, he said.

Arnold smiled suspiciously.

"How can you say that, Pastor Jørgensen! Why I know that you were away on Monday."

"But my dear friend! What sort of accusations are these! Amalie, you are my witness that I didn't go out of doors last Monday."

"No, my husband was really home. Who saw him someplace else?"

Arnold's burning eyes shifted searchingly back and forth between them for a moment, but at length it was not possible for him to doubt that their surprise was unfeigned. The surprise at once transplanted itself to him. His face suddenly became like a gaping mask, and unconsciously he looked toward Emmy. She was leaning back in her chair, fingering the fringe on its arm. At the same time, she looked out the window with an arrogant smile.

Arnold had to come forth with an explanation. He explained about the stranger's visit, about his false pretexts, his refusal to give any name, and ended with an exact description of his appearance. The pastor and his wife were both amazed. Pastor Jørgensen was a bit hurt.

"My dear Doctor Hojer–how could you be so naive? After the description you have given of the man, I do not understand how you could seriously assume him to be one of *my* friends!"

In the confusion of the moment, Arnold made excuses as well as he could. He explained that the pastor had once told him about a friend of his youth who had fallen from a wagon and who had since behaved rather strangely.

"Oh, poor Marius! But he has been dead for many years.–No, this was an impudent and shameless swindler! I have never heard the like of it!"

In the meanwhile, Emmy had brought out her crocheting and was working zealously, apparently without any particular interest in the conversation.

She is acting!–thought Arnold, who secretly watched her. That calm is affected! I know her! She is trying to reassure me.

The pastor swung about on the floor and continued to hold forth: "A most impudent swindler! In your place I would report the matter to the police instantly. Such a cheat deserves to be taken on the wing and to have his ears thoroughly boxed. Did you ever see the like! You'll see it was one of these intrusive and aimless commercial travelers, these disgusting traveling men who have begun to gad about in this part of the country too. That would be just like those fellows!"

Arnold took up this idea greedily in order to use it as a weapon. He said that he had suspected the fellow all the time. He had at first glance judged him to be a seedy actor or a cheap traveling entertainer, but he had to admit that the pastor was right in that he much more probably had been one of these traveling men who attracted bad taste through a certain superficial polish but were dreaded by all really cultivated persons. There had been something in the man of that mock elegance which is to be found in provincial hotels and in Copenhagen vaudeville.

Emmy sat there with her arrogant smile and felt quite sorry for him. But in a way, his vigorous attempts to conquer an imaginary rival were pleasing to her. The bloodthirsty words fell upon her heart like tokens of burning love. But how little he really understood her! Traveling salesman! Traveling singer! Oh Lord, that was of no consequence to her; she did not feel the slightest desire to meet that man again. It had been ridiculous when, in the confusion of the moment the other day, she had accused herself on account of that jolly pudge. To her he was and would remain what he had represented himself to be: Prince Carnival, who, for her sake, had once again left the realm of fairy tale and had crowned her its queen for a night.

Pastor Jørgensen pulled out his watch for the tenth time.

"Amalie—we must be going!"

At the same time, he plumped down in a chair to tell something peculiar that had just occurred to him. He could remember, he said, that in his childhood he had heard his parents talk about a very similar occurrence at the home of a forester someplace in Vendsyssel district. As he remembered it, a strange man had made his way into the bosom of the family under false pretenses and for several days had regaled himself as its guest.

"But the incident had a more tragic ending to be sure," he concluded, and stood up. "It was, I remember, the cause of an extremely saddening family catastrophe. If I do not err, the forester shot himself."

Arnold again did not know what to do with his eyes. While the pastor continued to talk, he fell for a moment into a state of deep pity for himself. Emmy understood at once. Despite her lowered eyelids, she saw through him and guessed all his melancholy thoughts. There broke forth a tender and tumultuous joy in her heart. Oh, how she wished that these outsiders would disappear so that she could be alone with him. She wanted to go straight to him and throw both arms about him so tightly that he would be defenseless before her kisses. And she would not release him before he had taken back all his ugly words and thoughts and really understood that she never had loved him more deeply and more thankfully than precisely during these last few days.

The pastor and his wife stayed half an hour longer; and when they finally were gone, the children came storming in from the dining room, and after them old Anna, who was grunting like a troll because she had had to wait with the supper—so the opportune moment for reconciliation was forfeited for the present. As soon as they had eaten, Arnold went into his own room. Emmy stood dejected, with tears in her eyes, and saw him close the door behind him.

In the evening, when the children had gone to bed and it was quiet in the house, Arnold from his room heard her at the piano. She played first a few scales and other exercises and then began suddenly, as if with a bold resolution, one of the same pieces the stranger had played that evening and precisely the one she had recently tried to rediscover by ear when Arnold had taken her by surprise.

What does this mean, he thought, disquieted. He began to be disturbed at her continued defiance.

This time she played the melody to the end almost without any hesitation. It was almost as if she must have practiced it during the intervening days. Now, no less, she began to hum along with the music. It was the song the stranger had sung about the devil, or whoever it might be, who one day assumed human shape and, disguised as a fool, journeyed about among humans and worked marvels. He still remembered the refrain:

And life goes on its stumbling way,
Turns wrong to right
Turns night to day,
Turns inside out and upside down,
Hurra, hurra, here comes the clown,
Once more to set the world aright.

He sat deep in thought with his hand under his chin while she continued to play and hum. It sounded like an attempt at seduction. Little by little a smile made its way to his bearded mouth—a pale and sad smile. Oh well, why not? As poor as he had become, he nevertheless did not wish to have his imaginary riches back again. Although he did not feel any less for Emmy, he was fond of her in another way now.—And he was, after all, not without flaws himself. She should be excused partly because he doubtless was not always easy to get along with. She had probably had good reason to complain about his irritability and lack of consideration.—In any case, they could not dispense with each other. Right now, more than ever, they stood in need of each other's support and would have to try to hold together with mutual indulgence unless they were to devastate life for each other.

He rose slowly in order to go to her. He wanted to tell her openly what he had felt and thought during these moments of quiet reflection. But he was no sooner in the door than he stopped suddenly. It was dark in the room. Only the candles on the piano were burning. On both sides they defined her silhouette in multifarious shapes on the floor and upon the walls. It was as if the room were populated by shadows.

Emmy continued to play; but he could see from her back that his coming made her very nervous. He went gingerly across the floor, and when he had stood for a moment behind her, he silently laid his hands upon her head. Continuing to play for a moment, she leaned back and looked blissfully into his eyes.

"Have you finally come!" she said softly.

Her hands fell. Like an emotionally overcome child, she leaned up against him while tears of joy trickled forth from under her closed eyelids.

VII

When Sørensen, after years of shrewd planning, had finally encircled Arnold Højer and stood poised to pass a judgment-day sentence on his authority in the region on the basis of the school's sewage system, Arnold, much to the schoolmaster's annoyance, smiled at him and his conspirators—and so kindly, with such charming mildness, that one would have to be a tenacious Jutlander like Lavst Sørensen not to feel embarrassed and ashamed.

"My dear friends!" said Arnold to the two representatives who ceremoniously appeared the day after Pastor Jørgensen's visit in order to inform him of the majority's decision in the matter. "Let us not concern ourselves with these bagatelles. I shall, of course, yield to the people's decision."

He carried his graciousness so far that he offered the two men coffee and cigars. Emmy poured for them herself and afterward gave them oranges and figs to take home to their children. Lavst Sørensen nevertheless found in this behavior a new reason to suspect them and to beat the drum for his own rustic accomplishments.

"Yes, it's what I've always said. That's the way these here city people are. They wobble back and forth according to what humor they are in. I pity that kind of folks."

His pronouncement won—for his purpose—a very convenient confirmation through the rumors which gradually filtered out regarding life in the doctor's house. There had already been talk about the strange carnival which had been held there; and people who recently had walked by in the evening had heard music and seen lights in all the windows as if there were company there every evening. Others had heard from the maids how the doctor and his wife one day kissed each other from morning till evening, the next day went about without speaking a word to each other, and finally again acted like newlyweds.

The curiosity now became further awakened with the report about the self-invited carnival guest and his merits. Since the doctor himself did not seem to want to take any steps to capture the swindler, the villagers became so much the more eager to institute a search themselves. At the inn, neither he nor the coachman had been seen. Neither in the nearest city nor in any other of the surrounding villages had they been able to get information. No one knew anything about a sleigh like the one they described. No one had seen it. It was as if it had disappeared into thin air.

As a result of all this, people were quick to agree that the young physician and his wife had undergone a deplorable change. Even the pastor and his family began to dissociate themselves from them after Emmy had appeared at a party in the parsonage with bared shoulders and on the same occasion had been more giddy and alluring than was proper for a married woman.

"I no longer understand those people," Pastor Jørgensen said, troubled. "It is as if all the good spirits had fled at once from the doctor's home, which used to be so pleasant and snug. It is all too clear that neither of them really feels happy anymore."

This last remark was in a way true enough. The friendly and chubby little elves which hitherto had hovered over each inhabitant of the little home were for the present in exile. Behind the festive procession of cupids and fauns which now housed there, there appeared more distinctly every day a weird company of shadows.

Even while Emmy walked about and hummed to herself, and was happy and played with the children, or looked out of the window to see if Arnold was coming, she could be overtaken by despondency, which made her feel indifferent toward everything. At other times, the slightest misfortune could bring her to tears. When Arnold was called out at night, she could not sleep. All sorts of dreadful mental representations, all sorts of self-accusations kept her awake, and fear made her superstitious. She would light her bedside lamp and sit up in bed trembling, with her hands about her knees. Every sound which reached her through the stillness of the night became a secret message which was sent to her from the spirit world. Or she would get up and fetch from a drawer the Bible which she had been given at her confirmation.

In the meanwhile, Arnold jolted cumbrously away out there in the wintry sleet. He too was wide awake. With a melancholy smile he sat in his carriage and thought of her with his heart full of tenderness and forgiveness. It was for them as in the first days of their love: with whatever bitterness they parted, as soon as they were away from each other they lived in continuous longing. Arnold thought at times that he could perceive physically how Emmy's thoughts followed him with kisses or tears.—But, contrarily, when they sat at home together, he often felt as if hundreds of miles were between them. No longer did it happen when they sat in his room and talked in the twilight that they began to laugh because each had sat and thought exactly the same way about the same thing. Her thoughts now went their own way, which he could not follow. Not even in moments of surrender under the intoxication of love was he quite sure of her. Yet how lovingly saddened she could be when he turned from her with that indifference or boredom which *she* did not feel. How sweetly she could thank him for every pleasure which he provided her! And how touching she could be with the lonely fear with which she awaited him on a night like this.

What more, after all, could he want? Why sigh over the quiet and secure paradise which he no longer possessed, when he did not feel himself wronged? He was content with his restless love—with his melancholy happiness. He was also thankful for his lonely hours which had given nature back to him as a confidante and had opened to him infinity's depth lying behind the stars of night, which bore the promise of eternity.—

Little by little both their minds were quieted. The trifling events of every day began again to interest them. Their life slid back into its accustomed track. Yet no matter how much their horizon gradually was narrowed again, it could long be observed in them that adventure had visited their home, and people continued to feel not quite at ease there. As Pastor Jørgensen said, it was as if there were a draft from all directions. One always had an impression of sitting in front of open doors.

There really was a certain constant uneasiness and fidgetiness in their behavior. It still happened that their frenzy had to have a chance to spend its fury for it still tended to flare up like a winter cold or like midsummer madness. Much oftener than Arnold—not to mention anyone else—suspected, Emmy's thoughts went astray and stole into the land of make-believe.

As an older woman with graying hair, she would often stand in solitude at the window with a dreamy, distant look and stare at the sunset and the vast, stormy sky where masses of ragged clouds constantly floated past from out of the west like a symbol of the restlessness of eternity.

Herman Bang

"Franz Pander" was first published in *Excentriske Noveller* (Eccentric Short Stories), in 1885. It has been reprinted in the edition of Bang's works, first issued in 1912, and in various collections of short stories. "Udvist af Tyskland" (Expelled from Germany) was included in *Ti Aar: Erindringer og Hændelser* (Ten Years: Memoirs and Happenings, 1891), reprinted in volume six of the collected works (1912: reprint ed. 1921). Though it is an autobiographical sketch, rather than a short story, it is exemplary of the narrator Bang.

That both selections from Bang take place on German soil is a bit misleading, for Bang's works are otherwise set in Denmark—although Bang himself spent a great deal of time abroad, chiefly in Germany, Austria, and Italy. He died in 1912, while traveling in the United States.

Franz Pander

Franz Pander's mother did washing for people. Her husband had been a carpenter and had drunk himself to death.

Perhaps that same carpenter was not Franz's father.

From time to time, Mrs. Pander took Franz's childish hand between her coarse hands, spread out his remarkably slender fingers, and marveled at the arched fingernails with their light pink cast. And she said, did Mrs. Pander, that that was the way *his* fingers had been and *his* fingernails. *He* was hardly the carpenter.

So perhaps Franz was illegitimate. He was an affectionate boy and ticklish, the way love-children are said to be. And he had feelings that none of the other boys along Kleine Dammstrasse shared.

His classmates called him "sissy." The name had been shouted by the class wit one day when the boys were swimming in the Elbe; *so* pale and delicate was Franz's body—and the name stuck.

It fitted well enough. Franz never played, never cursed, and did not smoke. Heaven knows what he actually did do. In front of the doorways along Kleine Dammstrasse, where the other boys pitched pennies and did cartwheels and squabbled and came to blows, he was never to be found. Nor was he often in his garret. Mother Pander could sit anxiously and wait for him by the hour in the evening before Mr. Franz came home.

"But where have you been, Franz?"

"Noplace."

"You never do anything."

"Did the consul's wife give you anything?"

"Yes, they had a party yesterday. It's a great delicacy."

Mrs. Pander took the pâté from between two plates in the oven. Franz ate it like a gourmet with little smacks of the tongue.

"They're champignons," he said. He loved the leftovers that his mother got in the various "good" homes where she did washing, and he inquired carefully about names and about how one ate every single thing. Ordinarily, when he had to be content with ordinary Dammstrasse food, Franz ate but little, and the little which he did eat he so drowned in pepper that Mrs. Pander sneezed when she just looked at it—the way he ruined good sausage.

During the afternoons Franz wandered about on Jungfernstieg. For hours he stood in front of the fancy store windows. Most of all he liked shiny, gilded bronze objects and decorators' exhibits where there were long pieces of flowing silk. There he stood and looked with his mouth open. But he could stand the longest gaping in front of the bookstore windows. He loved the reproductions of paintings. Pictures where men dressed in velvet sat at tables with women in silks and with draperies of red and with golden goblets on the table.

On the corner of the street called Neuerwall there was a picture: a dark woman in a low-cut dress of yellow satin, with two rows of pearls in her hair; she stretched out a plump, diamond-bedecked hand to a page in white, who was bowing deeply—in front of this picture Franz stood for hours, until he grew quite excited and had flushed cheeks. For now he was fourteen years old.

In winter evenings he read—all the novels where wild fantasy provides duchesses with brilliants about their proud necks and marquesses who languish in rosy orangeries.

Or he prowled about in the rich section along the Alster and looked up at the stories of buildings where the lights were burning for parties. He would wait at the portals until the carriages arrived, and his heart beat wildly at being so close to the ladies when they swept out of their carriages with lifted silk trains and to the gentlemen, slender, with their hair parted all the way down the back and with the fragrance of pomade.

Franz was crazy about everything that smelled good. Whatever Mrs. Pander could get her hands on, from time to time, and quite innocently (what does it matter if you take something from somebody who already has so much, she said once to Mrs. Fürst over the mangle) from this or that toilet table: Eau de Lubin or Ace Bouquet in a little bottle which she cautiously (goodness—when it was for the boy!) transported in her pocket; *this* Franz used to excess.

But then so did *he*—he whose hands and fingernails Franz had inherited.

And his whole figure for that matter. For Franz shot up and was growing into a handsome young man. Blue eyes—one couldn't tell whether they were melancholy or lethargic—a little mouth, actually too little for a man, with red lips, and a distinguished nose, straight, with nostrils which so easily trembled.

Slender and supple body.

That was the way he looked.

For that reason his mother wanted to have him in the men's clothing line. Mr. Schaltz had offered to take him.

"Nowadays you have to go in for smooth faces," said Mr. Schaltz, "and see them deck themselves out like princes by stealing from the till. Otherwise Heaven help us, you won't see a woman enter the store the entire day."

But Franz didn't want to go into the clothing line. One evening last winter when he was wandering along the Jungfernstieg, he had stopped in front of a big hotel. A club was holding a dance there. He had seen carriage after carriage roll in and the ladies descend, and in the lobby a swarm of waiters in their black cutaways and white neckties. How they bent down to the ladies when they removed the silk wraps from their shoulders and spoke to them in whispers and preceded them through the halls gleaming with light.

That's what Franz wanted to be.

He was to be an apprentice in a restaurant, a dismal hole in Schaumburgerstrasse where a couple of dozen beer-soaked regulars came to empty their steins. Franz suffered under the work: to rinse all these greasy beer glasses in the filthy water with *his* hands; and he suffered because of the air with its stench of bock beer and tobacco.

But he knew these years had to be, and he waited. He rejoiced because he saw that he grew more handsome every day. In the evening when he returned, dead tired, to his simple room, he could sit a long time with a lighted candle in front of his fragment of mirror and happily observe his own face. He tenderly nursed every bit of beauty which he possessed and, with the help of the tips he was given, he protected his hands by the use of rosewater and glycerine and the like.

The restaurateur's son came home for a visit. He was a journeyman waiter and was at present working in London.

He was full of stories about magnificent hotels with fathom-long mirrors, stairs of the purest marble, and portières of silk. And distinguished names and wines, the price of which Franz had never dreamed of, and lengthy rows of tables d'hôte along flower-bedecked sideboards . . .

Franz devoured every description.

And one morning when the restaurateur and his son were lolling on a sofa while the place was empty, the much-traveled son told stories from over there. Franz was washing up in his corner.

"One has one's happy moments—there in London.—" The waiter breathed cigar smoke out of his nostrils and pronounced London with an English accent. "One hell of an aristocracy, the English.—Wham, they look at you, a golden-haired miss, well dressed and erect—they look three or four times at your figure so your spine tingles and you feel the electricity when you get near them with a platter. . . . You have your routine and know how to do it. . . ."

The restaurateur and his son shared an intimate chuckle, and the son told about a couple of "hellishly lucky corkpullers."

"Of course he was handsome, John Jennings—a dashing chap—but that Lady Haverland herself ran away with him and took the whole works with her, as it were, so that Lord Haverland was left high and dry . . . by God I think that's . . . and Förner, he *married* a millionaire girl. He can thank his legs for that. . . ."

Franz had come out of his corner. With rolled-up shirt sleeves he stood a few steps from the counter and stared at the widely traveled son.

So it *did* happen, then.

Color came to his face and left again while he listened. The son suddenly turned around and looked at him.

"Say—fellow—you're dreaming . . ." he said, and continued to look at him. And in an undertone he said to his father, "Der Bub wird Glück haben."

The glasses rattled in Franz's dishpan that morning.

Franz was twenty years old when he reported at the Jungfernstieg Hotel.

The manager turned in his chair and looked at Franz's hands with the pointed fingernails while he pretended to be reading his letter of recommendation.

"Schön—eine dritte Stellung im Restaurant vacant. Sie können morgen anfangen."

When Franz, who had grown quite pale, was out the door, the manager said to the bookkeeper, who was alternately writing up accounts and picking his nose, "Na, ein netter Zugvogel—nicht?"

The first few days Franz was in a state of happy wonderment. He sneaked out of the restaurant onto the main stairway, eager to feel its carpets under his feet and to let his hand glide down along the black marble of the banister. He posted himself on the landing, where ladies with bouquets in their hands smiled and brushed past him. With his eyes he followed their figures, his heart palpitating until they disappeared around the corner; he saw their costumes and sensed the fragrance of their clothes more than he actually thought of the persons themselves.

He returned to the restaurant and went into the large table d'hôte dining room. He felt a sated sense of enjoyment in this room, with its subdued light which fell through the vast, many-colored window panes, its high arches borne by marble pillars, and its chandeliers as splendid as those in a church.

He was lost in thought until a fellow waiter aroused him. "Do you earn a lot by loafing here, man? We have a full house . . ."

He began serving again, bringing the courses on the menu to the tables and clearing them away, taking orders for the wines and opening the bottles. He luxuriously breathed in the aromas of the food, and, like a convalescent, was almost intoxicated by them. Without trying to discern what it was and without ascribing it to any one single cause, he went about in a state of euphoria, as though he were in love.

And in the evening, when the lights were finally extinguished in the dining rooms and the other waiters, tired as acrobats, hurried upstairs to go to sleep immediately, he stayed behind in the dark dining room; he could not tear himself away from the dimness in here, where the fountain splashed so softly in the basin among the great plants which stretched toward the darkened dome.

He wandered for a long time in the dim halls and hummed softly to himself, and when he finally went upstairs, where his roommates, hot and tired, lay asleep with open mouths, he lay awake for hours and felt a buzzing in his ears as if he were befuddled by wine.

Nevertheless, he was not tired during the day.

So it went at first. Then Franz grew accustomed to the new life, and there came a time when he felt very tired and always sleepy. His fellow workers were not interesting, either. They talked about their own affairs, about jobs they had had, and about how much they earned. They had girl friends among the maids or the kitchen help, and most of their time off they slept. About the guests they seldom spoke.

And the guests were what interested Franz.

Johanna, the maid on the second floor, was a tall, robust girl from Vienna who for some time had waylaid Franz every time he went out in the morning to tidy himself up; she liked to give him a few love pats and tickle his neck and exchange playful blows with him in one of the rooms where she was cleaning.

One day she pushed him down on an unmade bed, on the edge of which he had been sitting, and hit him in the face with a feather duster.

Suddenly she bent down and kissed the side of his throat while she held him.

Franz, turning pale, jumped up. "Let me go," he said. "I don't want to."

Johanna pushed him away angrily. "What are you thinking of, you silly fellow?" she said, and added scornfully, "Louis, wie du bist, Louis."

From that day on Johanna gave Franz a bad name among all the maids. They all harbored a silent fury toward Franz. They all actually wanted to have a chance at him, but *he* didn't see them. Never as much as a wink, the slightest push against a wall in the corridors, a pinch on the arm—nothing—just as if they weren't women at all. That's the way he was; but it was very irritating.

Franz didn't notice them at all. But on the evening of the same day that Johanna had thrown him on the bed, that same day something happened with Miss Ellinor in number 15.

"Fifteen" was a distinguished family, English—father, mother, and daughter. The family had lived there for some time. They always seated themselves at Franz's table, although there was a draft from the door there, and Miss Ellinor had a dozen questions to put and a dozen things to have brought to her, and first a bracelet fell and then a napkin fell right at her feet.

Franz was fascinated. It was as if something bound him to the little buffet table at the door. *There* he could see her profile. And he lingered over everything when he served that table: when he put down a glass, when he brought in a platter, when he spoke, when he bent down. It was almost a struggle to leave her, and he tingled all over when he but touched her.

His eyes were on her figure more often than he dared, and every time he approached her his heart stood still.

When she was not there, he was restless; he couldn't stay in any one place and he handled everything absentmindedly and he saw no one and nothing.

He felt a tug inside when she came *there* through the door. He didn't greet her—he greeted all the others. She smiled and a little breathlessly she asked for some soda water and a newspaper. She always managed to say a few words, and this time he had to remove some lint from her cape and help her with her parasol. It was always troublesome, wouldn't open and wouldn't close.

It was difficult for them to separate.

Franz believed and didn't believe, and he expected nothing and hoped for nothing. But he had to be near her.

If she would only sit *there* at his table all day and play like that, keeping time with her hands along the balustrade, as was her custom, while she hummed softly. If she would only do that.

But he grew more and more restless. And, scarcely noticeably, he began to get closer to her; just for a second he *had* to brush the corner of the table where her hand so often lay and to look long—so that she was conscious of it—at a certain bared place on her white throat.

Miss Ellinor pursed her little mouth and looked at him and laughed; she fondled her bony papa and looked at him and laughed; she put her hand next to Franz's on the table and looked at him and laughed.

He thought of only one thing: to touch her.

But gradually—for they stayed day after day—it was as if he was suffocating. His entire being was *absorbed* by her. Only her, day and night; her hand which had lain *there,* and the many times she had spoken to him—and there she had looked at him—yes certainly . . .

At night he couldn't sleep. He tossed and turned in the blankets. Kept doing that constantly. Her hand had lain *there—would* she touch him? *There* she had laughed, she had said *that*—he lay feverishly throughout the night, reliving the events of the day.

Suddenly when he was sitting up in bed, he looked at his roommates, who lay *there* fat and pale and tossed in the twilight of the dimmed gaslight. He found them so disgusting he could have kicked them.

Miss Ellinor was always the same. She played in the heat of his longing like a kitten in the gleam of light from a coal fire.

Then there was *that* evening. Franz was on duty on the first floor. *They* were out to a big party.

Franz wandered about and found not a minute of peace. He went in and out of the pantry and touched everything and accomplished nothing. Up the stairs and down the stairs he was driven without cessation. Finally they came. He recognized her voice—she had the habit of talking rather loudly in the corridors—and his heart stood still.

He took a light and went out in the corridor.

"You here?" she said.

"Yes—this evening." His voice failed him.

She looked at him briefly before she went in the door he had opened. "How so?" she asked.

"The other waiter is sick," he said, and lit the candelabra on the mantel.

Her father came in and went into the side room. The door was half open.

Miss Ellinor took off her necklace of precious stones in front of the mirror. Franz was about to go, but he remained standing with the light in his hand.

Then their eyes met in the mirror. A second later he had grasped her arm, and bent over and kissed her shoulder. He left the room and felt only that her pulse had throbbed under the kiss.

But then he was exhilarated by an overwhelming joy. He couldn't control himself; he laughed and sang. He spoke giddily with a fellow waiter who was drunk with sleep; he chattered and did not himself know what he was saying. In the corridors, he wandered about kicking boots so they went tumbling. Still in a festive spirit, he finally went upstairs; he undressed and carefully laid each piece of clothing next to the bed before crawling in. Then he lay quietly and smiled. But the next day Miss Ellinor left.

At breakfast, when he bent down to her, she looked him suddenly in the face and said, "We're leaving today."

"You're leaving?—Why?"

"Did you think that I was going to stay here?" and Miss Ellinor laughed.

There was no more conversation and they didn't see each other again.

For days Franz didn't know what to do with himself. He constantly relived his sparse memories and mechanically went through his duties at the same places where she no longer was.

A loud noise, a new face would arouse him suddenly, and for a moment he would see the dining room, the balustrade, the familiar tables, and the people around them. Then he would sink back into his lethargy, sick of everything and with a pain in his breast like a knife blade.

So it went for a time, until he was awakened one fine day and it suddenly seemed to him that all that was very far away and long ago and almost like something which had not happened to *him* and had only been dreamed.

And if he tried to capture the memories again, it was like traveling a long way, and if he did capture them he stood and marveled dully at his treasure.

He went back to cultivating himself again. *That* was past.

He went around performing his dull duties, limp and unthinking.

Gradually a waiter's hunger overtook him. He suffered as he brought the spiced dishes in and out. The aromas tempted him so much that he had to struggle to resist suddenly pouncing upon the platters and eating his fill hastily and greedily. He could feel a suppressed fury when he, with a smile designed for tips, recommended to the fastidious guests those dishes he himself might not taste; and from his corner he watched covetously every bite which the guests enjoyed.

But if he went down into the cellar—the waiters ate *there* in a room across from the laundry—where the air was heavy with the odor of boiled clothes, and the sweaty waiters took off their jackets and sat with unbuttoned vests over their food—he put down his spoon with sated disgust.

The waiters sat dully across from one another the length of the table and scarcely touched the heavy porridge and the frayed meat from the bouillon.

But when Franz came up into the dining room again, hunger screamed within him. And he, pale, carried the dishes back and forth and could taste them on his dry tongue.

Behind the door, on the landing, he would stuff a roulade in his mouth, tear the leg off a chicken, and gulp down gravy from a gravy dish, hastily and timidly. Every Tuesday evening, when he had a night off, he dressed and visited a restaurant where he was not known. He ran almost the entire way there, and he arrived excited and breathless with hunger. Then he forced himself to eat very slowly and to taste every mouthful sedately until, almost in a state of intoxication, he ordered more and more and ate hastily and to excess, in order for once to have enough and more than enough and sit with many half-empty glasses before him, slouched and half drunk with sluggish complacency. He then went home and, snoring, slept a heavy sleep.

One Tuesday evening he returned home early and sat down on a bench under the lights outside the hotel.

He was satiated and a bit giddy.

It had rained recently and there were a good many puddles on the sidewalk. Ladies tripped by with lifted skirts, nimbly avoiding the puddles.

Franz looked at the many feet—there the small of a leg, there a calf, there an ugly flat foot in a galosh. . . .

With curiosity he looked from the feet up at the swaying figures. The faces were so fresh under their veils.

He sought to catch one woman's attention. Wasn't *she* looking at him? He got up and followed her.

Uncertain, he walked behind her, his eyes glued on the slender figure and neck which showed under the upswept hair. . . . But she turned at Neuerwall and didn't look back. . . .

He returned, went in pursuit again uncertainly, following a slim figure which glided past with strikingly swaying hips. . . . She went into an entranceway and disappeared.

He wandered about again.

A streetwalker approached him. "What does my little friend have in mind?" she said.

Franz started and looked her in the face. Then he put his arm in hers and they walked along the sidewalk toward the light of the Alster pavillion. "Are you bored, darling?" the girl asked sweetly.

Suddenly Franz released her arm and started to run. "Hey!—Is he trying to make fun? . . ." the girl cried shrilly. "Do you know what you want, you scoundrel. . . . What a . . . takes up with a lady and runs off. . . ."

By this time Franz was out of earshot.

He ran almost the entire way home. Once there, he went to bed immediately. But the whole night through he tossed and slept poorly and restlessly.

He dreamed of Ellinor continually.

Toward morning he got up. He couldn't stay in bed any more. He was restless, and he had the feeling that something was in store for him. He wandered up and down the corridors, where it was beginning to get light. He stopped in front of the doors, and he picked up the women's shoes gently and looked at them for a long time. He put his hands into them and thought that he could feel the pleasant warmth of a foot.

That day he trembled when he even approached a woman. The fragrance from a bent neck surged up to him and drove the blood into his cheeks. It was as if he suddenly had a thousand eyes to see every beauty.

The delicate curling of the hair on a temple, the smooth roundness of a cheek, a hip and a waist to put one's arm around—or merely a light upon a bosom covered with taut satin—that was enough to tempt him.

On one of those days a heavy blonde came to the hotel. The first time she entered the restaurant she lifted her gold lorgnette—Franz saw her—and reviewed the waiters. Then she chose him.

Franz stepped forward and waited for her to order. He had his own way of standing, with his head slightly bent and his hands folded in front of him.

The lady's husband came and sat down.

"Well—we'll take the dinner," he said and turned around. "Hmm—hmm—" and he laughed. "That was a real Ganymede" he said. "Oh, um, waiter—two dinners . . ."

"Very well." Franz took a few steps.

Then the lady said, and not very softly, "His shirt front was the cleanest."

Franz spent three nights outside the lady's door, pressed in the doorway like a thief, fearful of meeting the shoe polishers, who went through the corridors with their baskets; his teeth chattered with cold.

He crept out of his bed, which burned beneath him; he sat in a pantry; he opened the window in order to get air to breathe. He cursed himself, and his mind had no other thought than desire.

He resurrected her indifferent glances in his thoughts and he invested them with promise, so stupidly that he laughed at it himself. He saw her figure and he heard her voice. He saw her fingers, round as white snakes. And he went back to her door and he stood there until daybreak. He knew that it was absolutely crazy, but he remained.

And when she left, another came. There was no cessation. It was scarcely women he loved; it was a mouth, a throat, a beauty spot, a body. He spied on every woman. He hoped anew with every one. He knew he was offering himself too visibly. All his handsome features—and how he compared them with those of other men, *their* men—he was proffering. But they didn't see him at all.

He stood next to them, like a *thing*. Trotted off with platters and napkins—simply an *object*—he realized it himself.

But at night came brief memories of a glance toward him, a warm hand when he received a tip. And this drop of nectar was enough to excite him, to make his thirst seem loathsome . . .

Frequently Franz stole out of the restaurant for a hasty trip through the corridors. He listened at doors. He looked through keyholes.

At the tables d'hôte, where the gentlemen and ladies sat in rows, it might happen that a man who, with a smile, had leaned toward the lady next to him, would withdraw somewhat brusquely, having an odd feeling at the sight of the pale face above the platter when

Franz appeared. It was as if the fellow had *hatred* in his eyes.

After dinner, at coffee, it might happen that a gentleman, after he had lighted his cigar, would turn to his wife or his sister. "Devilishly handsome fellow," he would say. Franz heard it, and she would lift her eyes and look at him as if he were a clothes rack and say, "Oh yes—for a roué."

That's the way it went day after day.

He thought of nothing except *that.*

Like a pickpocket, he touched them casually; they didn't even notice. He was almost insolent; they didn't even *feel* it.

And when the day had dragged past and become evening and the dining room was empty, Franz would stand for hours leaning motionless on the balustrade, staring, and looking pale under the electric light.

Despair was churning in his mind—an impotent fury which searched for an answer and found none and didn't know where it should turn.

Occasionally he went home. He thought it helped.

Mrs. Pander sat and wept quietly.

"He sits there," she said to the woman at the mangle, "and looks like misery itself and doesn't say a single word. You know what it is . . . yes, but . . . you know what it is . . ."

He didn't want to have the light turned on—the dark was better. He took off his jacket silently and he sat in the old sofa in the corner. Mrs. Pander took a chair and sat down in front of him.

She took his hands between hers and caressed them softly and he, tired and silent, smiled at her and put his head on her shoulder.

"What is it, my boy—little boy—what is wrong with my boy?"

He wrung his hands and didn't answer. And Mrs. Pander felt his forehead burning against her shoulder and said again with a voice which her weeping made almost incomprehensible, "What's wrong with you, my boy—little boy—what have they done to you?"

When Franz had gone, Mrs. Pander damned all females to the woman at the mangle. "It's their fault, *that* riffraff—good Lord—and he didn't get it from strangers."

One Tuesday evening Franz went to the theater to see an operetta.

It was a Turkish story about a princess.

There was a fat eunuch with pillows on his stomach. When he tried to make love, the entire audience shrieked. They called him back on stage again and again, and he repeated his gestures ever more boldly and sang his ditty,

> Aber—es hat keinen Wert—
> Es hat keinen Wert.

Franz sat in the darkness in a box. He leaned back against the wall and wept.

When the act was over he left.

He walked obliquely toward the Gänsemarkt and into one of the alleys in that section of town. He stayed there all night.

But when he wakened toward morning and saw her next to him in the twilight, he jumped up and ran out.

His feeling of disgust was so strong that he felt as if he might disgorge himself. He was feverish and his head hurt. He groaned with nausea.

He went home, but he didn't want to go to bed. He crept down to the restaurant by the back stairs.

It had begun to get light, and a gray twilight came through the glass roof.

Franz sat down on the stone stairs with his head in his hands.

While he sat here quietly in front of the dining room which was witness to his life, everything slid into a deep, bottomless pit of indescribable loathing.

He looked along the balustrade—the chairs were put up on the tables and the dirty tablecloths were spread out over them; the artificial palms bristled lifelessly in their majolica pots.

Franz didn't have a thought and felt no pain. But into his mind there came something like a stupified amazement that this was life.

The lamplighter had forgotten his tall ladder the day before when he had extinguished the lights. Franz stood on one of the rungs when he strung himself to a crossbar over the door. The cleaning women found him and there was a great commotion, and the night porter was called. Franz looked horrible with his tongue protruding from his mouth; he was still warm.

The hotel director came down in his nightclothes, cursing so loudly that it resounded in the dining room. A couple of fellow waiters carried Franz up to the fourth floor to a baggage room.

They cleared luggage and hatboxes off a table and laid him *there* among the luggage. A couple of potato peelers washed the corpse and covered it with a sheet.

Late in the morning Johanna came in. She wanted to see him. She lifted the sheet slowly, leaving only the head covered. She didn't cry but looked at him silently.

He was white as marble; she had never seen anything so beautiful.

And while she looked at the corpse on which so much affection had been lavished, Johanna—she didn't herself know why—lifted her clenched hand toward Heaven.

Expelled from Germany

Without being a menace to society, I had lived six weeks in a hotel, when, on the first of January, I moved into a private home, and then the troubles began.

The registration form passed from my landlady into the hands of the police of the imperial city of Berlin.

One fine morning there appeared at my lodging a youngish and well-dressed person, who put a number of rather intimate questions to me concerning my activities and various circumstances of my life, which somewhat surprised me. When I meekly expressed my astonishment, he most politely presented a little badge and said that it was after all reasonable that the *police* were a bit interested in foreign arrivals like me.

He also asked me in an extremely amiable manner —"it was a formality, only a formality"—just to jot down on a little piece of paper the publications for which I wrote.

For which I wrote? Well, the man could not know that the list would be *very* long.

I jotted down—Danish newspapers, Swedish newspapers, German newspapers . . .

The pleasant man asked me kindly whether I did not also write for Norwegian newspapers.

I answered yes, and added a Christiania newspaper to the list.

The friendly person wondered whether that was perhaps the only Norwegian newspaper . . .

No, I answered, there was also one other . . .

"I see . . ."

It wasn't apparent that this particularly interested the gloved man. But he asked me anyway, as a matter of routine—the whole thing was after all "a formality" —to add the name of that newspaper too.

Which I did, and wrote *Bergens Tidende.*

The exemplary gentleman thanked me. He didn't need more newspapers now. He said a few words about "such an exhausting occupation" and stuck the paper in his pocket: that was sufficient.

He was very pleasant, as I have said, but nonetheless, he did not shake hands when he left.

Two days later, when I came home from the theater, my landlady notified me that an unusual gentleman had been to see me; he had absolutely insisted on waiting for me and had waited three hours.

But I had been at the Deutsches Theater, where they are reluctant to cut too much out of Schiller, and I had seen *Don Carlos,* so that at last it had been too much even for the strange gentleman, and he had gone away again.

The next morning I was awakened from a sound sleep: the mysterious gentleman was there again.

I requested that he kindly come when decent people got up. *Now* I was sleeping.

But my landlady said that certainly wouldn't do. For he was, she thought, from the police.

I sat up in bed. From the police? "What the devil does he want?" I asked.

Well, said my landlady, who was quite frightened, I would probably find out now when I came down—for the mysterious gentleman was waiting. He wouldn't leave.

He would wait.

Quite right—the gentleman was waiting.

He asked me—he was not quite as polite as the man of the other day—to take the matter calmly, but told me that I must report at the police station.

At the main police station.

I said I would come in the course of one hour.

But he insisted that he must accompany me—and at once.

I won't say that I exactly liked the situation, while I got dressed in the bedroom and he waited with his legs crossed in a chair in my sitting room.

When we got down to the street door, he asked me if I possibly wanted to have a cab.

Yes, thanks.

Whether I used first- or second-class cabs.

We got a first-class cab, and the persistent gentleman got in beside me.

I asked just what I had done. The man replied, "There is no use asking. It does not concern me."

So I arrived at the main police station somewhat unclear about the nature of my offense.

I went through many corridors and many rooms—my man was at my side; many officials were sitting at many desks—the man was at my side.

At last I entered a room where I was to wait. It was a detention area for vagrants. There on a wooden bench were already sitting two fellows of not quite irreproachable appearance.

The gentleman from the cab handed me over to the room's attendant and withdrew.

I asked again exactly why I was here. And the new gentleman replied again, "There is no use in asking. It does not concern me."

Whereupon I paced the floor for an hour, during which there came more and more vagrants, until the air became not altogether pleasant.

At last I asked how long I'd likely have to wait.

The new gentleman answered that there was nobody there who would know.

And I waited again—half an hour.

Then the gentleman from the cab came back and took me with him.

"Now you will find out," he said.

I already felt as if I were a Russian about to be sent to Siberia.

I was led into a new room and again waited—this time in front of a counter.

Behind the counter were working probably twenty gentlemen, each in front of his ledger.

One of these gentlemen finally pushed forward toward me, carrying a large document in his hand. I saw there was something printed on it. The gentleman asked me whether I was Herman Bang, and when I affirmed this, he read out my expulsion order to me.

I was expelled from the kingdom of Prussia.

I permitted myself to ask in a low voice about the reasons. The gentleman only continued to read.

I was to leave Berlin within twenty-four hours, and if after that time I was found inside the kingdom, I would, after imprisonment, be transported to the border.

When he had finished reading, I again asked about the reasons. The gentleman with the document replied very brusquely, "Sign, please. . . . No reasons are given here."

I think I probably was supposed to sign "for information only," so to speak.

I pointed out that after all I was not some journeyman carpenter, and that an expulsion would evoke considerable publicity. The gentleman with the paper appeared rather cold-blooded about publicity. Handing me the pen, he said, "Oh, it won't be so bad."

After receiving forty-eight hours to prepare for departure, I signed.

During the whole ceremony, not one of the nineteen at the desks had so much as raised his eyes. Prussian officials do not listen to what does not concern them. I once visited a ministry in St. Petersburg. There, at every turn of the corridors, a couple of officials stood chatting. There were a hundred people who obligingly wanted to give us information and not one who knew anything whatsoever. One official seemed never to be able to find another one. Each time we entered a new room, everybody would look up, and a whole crowd would collect to give us information.

An old gentleman who was something like a head clerk left his office and accompanied me through half the building.

He asked me about Denmark's geographical situation and detained me in the cold corridors for over an hour. He was an amateur geographer.

He took a kind of cap off his head and said time after time, while he swung it in the air, "People certainly ought to be acquainted with the world they live in."

In Berlin's police headquarters, things are not the same as in St. Petersburg. A Prussian official is a sentinel in front of his ledger, and a Brandenburg sentinel guards his door and only his door; it is forbidden for him to speak.

After receiving the expulsion order, I drove over to the Danish envoy. He would do whatever he could and, in any case, would find out what was behind it.

We found out what it was: it was distressing. And Count Herbert Bismarck himself placed it on the table before the envoy, in the form of a Bergen feature article.

After that, all protests were silenced; the article was too eloquent. It did not seem even to me that I had any grounds whatsoever for complaint. Moreover, the article had been sent in by the German consul in Bergen and had been waiting for a long time—in its place and provided with a number—in the Foreign Ministry along with mountains of other Scandinavian documents.

For they collect all sorts of printed matter most conscientiously *there* in Berlin.

Amazingly conscientiously, say those who know about it.

A year or so after my expulsion, on the occasion of some very frank utterances at a couple of political meetings here at home—utterances that were reported in the newspapers—I wrote that my countrymen should perhaps speak a bit more softly. For, after all, there was only a wall between us and Germany, and "walls can have ears."

The remark was violently derided. If they had known *who* had pronounced it, they would perhaps have "laughed" a bit less loudly.

My only hope was that my expulsion could proceed quietly. I didn't find the occasion really well-chosen for making a fuss. After all, I knew that sooner or later *Bergens Tidende* would reach Berlin—in translation.

I wanted only to find out whether I could possibly reside unmolested somewhere else in Germany. Count Herbert Bismarck thought I probably could. And I decided to go to Meiningen. I made my farewell visit to the *Berliner Tageblatt.*

I went for the last time up the steps of the world-famous newspaper. It was Arthur Levysohn who had been most instrumental in my coming to Berlin. He had followed my work at home and thought that there would be a place in Berlin for me. I was to be the paper's theater critic. My first articles had already been printed.

Now there was nothing else to do but say good-bye. I "took my hat"—and left.

My last evening in Berlin I drove with a Danish friend up Unter den Linden. Beautiful and vast it lay there, its torrents of humanity poured forth—one of the great arteries of human life.

My Danish friend stood up in the coach. He looked down toward the distant Brandenburg Gate with its triumphal span; everything was bathed in light—everything, people and palaces.

"Beautiful, lovely city," he said. And we sat silent for a long time.

"Beautiful, lovely city."

Yes, here was the *grand monde,* and now Mr. H. B. was going home to his nook, a *new* nook.

I set out the next morning.

It is not all that easy to get to Meiningen. You must change trains several times, and you end up on a narrow-gauge railroad in a train with one passenger coach and one freight car.

On this train you then jog along at a deliberate pace, and have the impression of having turned off into one of the world's byways.

But it was pleasant and peaceful there in Meiningen. People knew what had happened to me, but pretended they didn't.

The days passed. The court players went to rehearsal and returned from rehearsal to drink their beer at the hotel. Their promenades were the most important events of the day. People followed them with their eyes through the whole town. The ducal seat has only one street, where all the court purveyors' doors rust quietly on their hinges.

In the evening the whole town was at the theater.

The duke was at the front in his box, and the people listened. They knew the repertory by heart and rejoiced loudly.

It might be late at night before one returned home. Costume changes were so abundant at the Meiningen theater.

The worthy people of Thuringia would stroll homeward, noisily happy. They enjoyed the troupe's world renown as if it were their own. Their favorite play was

Wilhelm Tell. In that play the privy councillor roars as if avalanches were rolling down into the wings.

"Gott, Gott," the townspeople would say, "heute hat er denn brav gedonnert."

They were, moreover, pleased with Lindner's *A Blood Wedding.* For that performance, the garrison was ordered out and laid siege to the theater. In the castle park they fired on command amid loud cheers.

On the stage, Mme. Olga Lorenz looked from a window at the ravaged Paris: the din in the castle park was meant to be the Massacre of St. Bartholomew.

Every Sunday all the youth of the duchy arrived under colors. They marched into the theater like Grundtvigians to a shooting match.

There were also concerts: Hans von Bülow's farewell concert. Hans von Bülow, as is well known, was conductor of the court orchestra, but in this position he was not always exactly in agreement with His Highness.

On the contrary, he very often had his own opinions, which he was in the habit of expressing very loudly.

The outstanding conductor had, from the podium at a concert in Cologne, openly upbraided His Highness and had cheerfully permitted his abusive words to be reported. His resignation had therefore been graciously accepted.

He was now to conduct a farewell concert. The whole town trembled in anticipation. Herr von Bülow, it was thought, would not spare his public at his farewell.

Herr von Bülow appeared on the podium at ten minutes before seven. It was evident that this evening he wanted to begin on the stroke of seven, for His Highness was sometimes a single minute late.

But this evening Duke Georg had looked at his pocket watch just as precisely as had Dr. von Bülow, and had entered his box at one minute before seven.

Herr von Bülow acted as though he did not see him. The rest of the audience he looked over with an eye like that of a Prussian corporal inspecting his unit.

The attitude of the public was such that the departing conductor found no occasion for remarks.

His Highness applauded heartily.

One fine day I received a newspaper from Hamburg. It contained a feature article from a correspondent in Copenhagen. I was the subject of the article. I may venture to say that not a single unpleasantness uttered on this subject in a corner of a Danish café was omitted in this account. The writer conscientiously found a place for everything, even the misfortunes that had befallen my deceased relatives.

For those who believed all this, I suppose I could not but look like a dangerous person.

And why shouldn't they *believe* it in a foreign country, when there was someone who would *write* it in my own?

I thought immediately when I read it: Now you'll be expelled here, too.

And so I was—extremely quickly.

A couple of days afterward came a summons. I was to report to the mayor's office. He wished to see me the next morning at eight o'clock. German officials are addicted to starting things off at an early morning hour.

I reported and saw immediately that the papers were in order. They lay completed at His Honor's side.

It turned out that I was to be expelled from said city of Meiningen with the customary twenty-four hours' notice.

I declared that I could not possibly leave so quickly. The mayor suggested that it was not so far to the border *there* in the duchy, which was indeed the case. But I would, I thought, have to go a little farther than to Gotha.

I went to the prime minister.

He was a plain, good-natured man, who often at twilight sat in the hotel café with his stein.

I went to see him now in the ministry. It most resembled a fair-sized freight office. The prime minister was sitting in his office—the chairs were upholstered with horsehair—at an old secretary.

I presented my case and asked about the reason for my expulsion. I had, after all, been told in Berlin that I would be able to live undisturbed in Meiningen.

The prime minister said, "I don't know the reasons. Wir haben nur Befehl aus Berlin."

And, lowering his voice imperceptibly, he said, "Here we can do nothing."

The old man got up and turned toward the window, as if he were suddenly moved. And after a short silence he said, "Here too are parents whose sons fell at Langensalza."

But he did grant me two days and we parted with a handshake.

The next morning, however, a policeman—I believe the ducal residence has two—appeared at my bedside to remind me, at the mayor's behest, about my departure. I was *now* feared as a fragment of revolution in the duchy.

When I departed, the policeman was present on the platform—in plain clothes.

I left for Munich.

I had been advised to select a kingdom as a place of residence.

I arrived in Munich in the evening. I went to a hotel where for many years I had been in the habit of staying. The next morning I was awakened by the hall porter, who was greatly alarmed.

The police had been there to inquire of my whereabouts.

Already, I thought, and realized that Munich would, after all, scarcely be suited for my lasting asylum.

I set my departure for around noon.

I was convinced that there was no time to lose.

First I went out to see Henrik Ibsen, who was living in a strangely homeless fashion amid a profusion of rented furniture, which several family portraits on the walls stared at with confused or oddly astonished eyes. The master shook his gray head at my story and said again and again, "What have we come to—what indeed have we come to!"

At two o'clock I left on the eastbound express. I found it expedient to retreat from the Hohenzollerns and visit the Habsburg monarchy. I settled down in Vienna.

For four or five months I lived completely undisturbed. One of the very few people I knew was the Danish envoy, about whom I—like all Danes, I'm sure—cherish the most affectionate and friendliest memory.

I had moved out to Hernals and lived there quite alone. I saw literally no one for weeks, but worked and worked on my novel *By the Wayside.* My landlady was a widow with six children; the whole lot lived in a kitchen with adjoining dining room.

It struck me that later there was a constant succession of men in this dining room.

The landlady told me they were suitors.

Her husband was hardly cold in his grave, and she was frenetically submitting marriage offers at all the newspaper offices.

She would say, "What can a person do who is left all alone?"

For a long time she insisted that the gentlemen in the dining room were suitors, as I have said.

But one fine day she informed me in confidence that they were "detectives." They questioned her every day about me.

What did they want with me, I asked.

Well, she didn't know. But they looked through my papers when I was not at home.

I asked her whether they could read them.

No, they couldn't. But they always asked if I went out at night, and if I had Russian visitors.

I understood *now* I was on the way to becoming an out-and-out nihilist.

I notified the Danish envoy, and he went to the chief of police. Quite right—I was thought to be a suspicious person.

Inquiry was made as to what I had done. But about that I was given no information. It was simply thought that my presence was rather superfluous in Vienna. Having imparted this information, the police chief enveloped himself in a cloud of secrecy.

Austrian police are fond of having their secrets. They are still operating under the tradition of Prince Metternich.

For these police I naturally couldn't help being a choice morsel. They could appropriately dream up anything and everything precisely because there was nothing there.

Morning and evening the landlady made her report in her dining room. I fell over detectives at my street door.

The landlady feathered her nest. She claimed that she had kept her rent money in a bureau in my sitting room. The rent money, she said, had now disappeared.

Why, I knew myself, she said to me with such heartfelt gentleness, that no one came into my room.

Why, *she* would be reluctant to involve the police in the matter . . .

The gentleman really has enough—more than enough anyway . . .

Her expression depicted in understanding sympathy *everything* that I undoubtedly "had."

But she was a poor woman, who had to have her rent money.

I understood it, she had to have her rent money.

It was twenty guilders. My purse became lighter by that amount.

And a couple of days later I left for Prague. It had been thought that I would be less troublesome in the provinces.

I rented an apartment in a suburb, and on Saturday evening I moved in. On Sunday morning a police officer rang the bell.

Whether I was Mr. so-and-so?

Yes (I had heard that song before), I was Mr. so-and-so.

Then there was a summons, said the man.

I didn't doubt it, and took the papers.

I reported in accordance with the summons. At last I had fallen into the hands of a couple of officials who knew their duty and took it seriously.

Here they had no intention of letting a criminal die a sinner.

For the time being, I was permitted to wait on the bench of the accused for an hour. I sat between two gentlemen who had been arrested for begging. When I was finally admitted I realized that now I had come to the right parties.

These two gentlemen were not men who let a secret get by them. They were much too fond of secrets for that to happen. And they were as ingenious as public officials in an operetta.

They treated me as if I were certain of the gallows, and began by asserting that I had forged my passport.

The senior official, who had a very red nose, declared importantly that they knew me.

I answered meekly that this was apparently more than I myself did.

The senior official asked me earnestly to keep my wittiness to myself: they *had* received their report.

I asked what was in that report.

The senior official replied only that the report was from Vienna.

He pronounced this city's name as if I had killed a significant proportion of my unfortunate family right in Kärntner-Ring.

I said that I understood that it must have come from Vienna.

The official smiled and said with a strong emphasis, "So you do understand that?"

The junior official entered my confession in a ledger.

I realized that I now was hopelessly suspicious.

I maintained my innocence, however.

"My good man," said the official, "one does not send in a report about innocent persons."

"We know you."

The junior official signified by a nod that he, at least, knew me through and through.

But it was clear that if I was known, the secret was not known. And they *wanted* to know it. They *would* yet get to know it.

They interrogated me for an hour and three quarters.

By that time the two gentlemen had filled seven folio sheets with confessions, and I was looked upon as a hardened criminal.

The older gentleman told me that in words that left nothing to be desired in the direction of candor. And as I left, he said that I would hear from him.

That I did: every morning for eight days there was a police officer at my door.

Every other day I received summonses. The yellow papers were common knowledge throughout the house. The tenants, I must confess, did not exactly throng to make my acquaintance.

It was the middle of summer. The sun made the courtrooms sweltering. The two officials sweated blood from pious and feverish zeal; never have officials been more foul-mouthed.

One day I received a summons from the office of the chief of police. I now accepted without emotion everything that happened. I had become accustomed to the police desk.

I was led in to a very distinguished-looking gentleman, who treated me as if I were a Polish Jew selling floor mats.

I was informed that once again a report had arrived from Vienna.

I answered that I just didn't understand what there was to report.

He announced brusquely that "there could not be reports if I had not done something."

I asked, tired and desperate—for now it was surely the thousandth time—what crime I had committed. And the man replied, "If we knew that, Mr. what's-your-name, we would certainly not be interrogating you."

I did not tell the man that he was going around in a circle. I didn't say anything at all. It would have been useless. But it is, I can vividly imagine, at such moments that arrested creatures invent crimes in order at least to put an end to it.

The police prefect sent me away after having recommended caution to me.

Moreover, the house where I lived was festooned with detectives. They wished especially to learn whether I received nocturnal visits. I received no visits either night or day.

Viennese acquaintances advised me to go home. Austrian police were difficult when they had once got something in their heads; that's the way they were.

"They were police who didn't give up easily."

That I had to concede.

But I still did not want to go home until I could do it with my novel *Stucco* in my pocket. So I remained for another year. The police continued to shower me with attention. But as to what was in the "reports" they never informed me.

They undoubtedly had their reasons.

Well, however that may be—persistent such police must *surely* be called.

Notes

Maser

34 *The Raven* · *Ravnen* (1867) contains the prehistory of "Maser." On a voyage to South America, Ferdinand Carøe meets Mr. Philpots and saves his life. Philpots tells him of his youth in Denmark, and of Simon Levi, who gave Philpots all his money in order to enable him to escape, after having been mistakenly suspected of wrongdoing. Now a wealthy man, Philpots gives Carøe a gold coin to repay Simon Levi. Subsequently, Carøe also saves the life of Simon Levi, who is then instrumental in unmasking the villain who is persecuting the Carøe family. The Carøes are able to maintain control of the factory (mentioned in "Maser") which they had established.

37 chick peas · garbanzos

62 Amalienborg · the royal residence in Copenhagen

65 society of wholesale dealers · Membership in the prestigious "Grosserer-Societet" enables a man to use the

title *Grosserer* even today. As a sign of respect, the surgeon later in the story addresses Simon Levi as "Hr. Grosserer," here translated as "Mr. Levi, sir."

Mogens

83 counselor · In the late nineteenth century, the title of *Justitsraad*, granted by the crown, was purely honorary

county official · The *Sognefoged*, appointed by the *Amtmand* (*infra*), performed the functions of a constable within the area of a parish (*Sogn*).

86 The Story of Sir Peter · "Historien om Ridder Peder med Sølvnøglen." The Danish chapbook about Fair Magelona was first published in 1583. The thirty-second of thirty-five editions was issued in 1871 and is the only one to reverse the title as Jacobsen has it: *En meget smuk Historie om Ridder Peder med Sølvnøglen en Grevesøn af Provence og Den skjønne Magelone . . .*

Vigoleis · "Vigoleis med Guldhjulet." The first known edition, published in 1656, identifies it as translated from a German translation of the French: *En smuck lystig Historie/ Om den berømmelige Ridder oc Heldt Her Viegoleis med Guld Hiulet. . . .* A thirteenth edition of the chapbook appeared in 1855.

Bryde the Marksman · "Skytten Bryde." Danish chapbook, *Ærens Tornevej for en Skytte navnlig Bryde*, dating from 1710.

87 Aren't you a student? · *Student* is a Danish appellation which indicates that a person has passed the maturation examination that is a prerequisite for matriculation at an institution of higher learning.

88 district magistrate · *Amtmand*. The governing official (appointed by the crown) of one of the nineteen administrative districts into which Denmark is divided.

89 When I reach my majority · In the nineteenth century, a Dane did not reach legal majority until the age of twenty-five.

Elverhøj · "Elfin Hill" (1828), an operetta by Johan Ludvig Heiberg (1791–1860), has consistently been the most popular piece given at the Royal Theater in Copenhagen.

95 "To Babylon, to Babylon" · The title seems to be Jacobsen's invention. No such poem has been identified.

Arup Ford · Actually a small pond just north of the hamlet of Arup in northern Jutland, about seven miles east-northeast of Thisted (Jacobsen's home)

Jannerup · Village west of Thisted in northwest Jutland

Himmerland · A district in northeastern Jutland (later the setting for Johannes J. Jensen's *Himmerlandshistorier*)

109 Mönsted · village west of the city of Viborg in Jutland

114 Bredbjerg, Grönhöj · descriptive place-names: "Broad hill, green height." Each occurs separately in Jutland.

The Royal Guest

144 Jerrild · An invented place-name

186 Vendsyssel · Northernmost district of the Jutland peninsula

Franz Pander

197 Kleine Dammstrasse · This street name is Bang's invention.

198 Jungfernstieg · Street running along the Alster basin in central Hamburg; site of the best hotels and shops

199 Neuerwall · Street which runs at right angles into the (alter) Jungfernstieg

201 Schaumburgerstrasse · The allusion is presumably to Schauenburgerstrasse, which ran between the Exchange and the Johanneum in central Hamburg.

202 "Der Bub wird Glück haben" · "That lad will make out all right."

Jungfernstieg Hotel · There were several hotels along the Jungfernstieg; of these the most exclusive was the Hamburger Hof, to which Bang may be alluding

203 "Schön—eine dritte Stellung im Restaurant vacant. Sie können morgen anfangen." · "Fine, the third-line position in the restaurant is open. You can begin tomorrow."

"Na, ein netter Zugvogel—nicht?" · "Well, a nice bird of passage, isn't he?"

205 "Louis, wie du bist Louis" · "Louis, the way you are, Louis." "Louis" was a word for pimp.

215 "Aber—es hat keinen Wert—" · "But there's no use."

Gänsemarkt · Square in the northwest part of downtown Hamburg

Expelled from Germany

219 *Bergens Tidende* · Newspaper of Bergen, Norway, in which Bang had published on 1 October 1885 an article that mentioned members of the Kaiser's family in an uncomplimentary fashion. Bang had gone to Berlin in December 1885 and was forced to leave in mid-January.

223 the Danish envoy (in Berlin) · Carl Rudolph Emil Vind (1829–1906) was the Danish envoy in Berlin 1884–1902.

Count Herbert Bismarck · Herbert von Bismarck (1849–1904), son of Otto von Bismarck, was Secretary of the Foreign Office in Berlin from 1886 to 1890.

224 Arthur Levysohn · (1841–1908). Foreign editor of *Neues Wiener Tageblatt* prior to his expulsion from Vienna in 1875 for his political views. He was subse-

quently on the staff of the *Berliner Tageblatt* and was editor-in-chief from 1882 until 1906.

225 Meiningen · Bang went to Meiningen, which was then famous for its theater, and there met the actor Max Eisfeld (pseudonym for Max Appel, 1863–1935), with whom he went to Vienna and then to Prague. Viennese police records show that he was under surveillance for homosexual activity.

the Duke · Georg II von Sachsen-Meiningen (1826–1914). After the death of two wives, he contracted a morganatic marriage with the Meiningen actress Ellen Franz (Helene, Freifrau von Heldburg) in 1873.

226 the privy councillor · Ludwig Chronegk (1837–91), director of the Meiningen troupe from 1871 until his death, bore the title *Hofrat.*

"Gott, Gott . . . heute hat er denn brav gedonnert" · "Lord, Lord . . . today he thundered right well."

A Blood Wedding · *Die Bluthochzeit: Ein geschichtliches Trauerspiel in 4 Acten* by Albert Lindner (1831–88). The play was published as fascicles 29–30 of *Repertoir des herzoglichen Meiningen'schen Hof-Theaters* (Leipzig: F. Conrad, 1887).

Mme. Olga Lorenz · (d. 1920), actress married to Alexander Otto. She did not come to Meiningen until 1887.

Grundtvigians · Humorous reference to the followers of the Danish clergyman N. F. S. Grundtvig (1783–1872), poet, theologian, politician, and instigator of the folk high school movement

Hans von Bülow · Hans Guido Freiherr von Bülow (1830–94), pianist and conductor, held the post of "Hofmusikintendant" in Meiningen from 1880 until his resignation in 1885. He is remembered today as the first husband of Cosima Liszt, who left him for Richard Wagner in 1869.

228 the prime minister · Baron Albrecht Otto von Giseke.

"Wir haben nur Befehl aus Berlin" · "We only have orders from Berlin."

Langensalza · Bad Langensalza, near Erfurt, was the site of the victory of Prussian over Hannoverian troops on 29 June 1866.

229 the Danish envoy (in Vienna) · Count Joachim Sigismund Ditlev Knuth (1835–1905)

Hernals · Western suburb of Vienna (now District 17 of the Viennese municipality)

By the Wayside · Bang's novel *Ved Vejen* (1886)

234 *Stucco* · Bang's novel *Stuk* (1887)